THE SECRET OF THE DASHING DETECTIVE

REMINGTONS OF THE REGENCY BOOK 2

ELLIE ST. CLAIR

CONTENTS

Chapter 1	1
Chapter 2	10
Chapter 3	19
Chapter 4	27
Chapter 5	36
Chapter 6	43
Chapter 7	51
Chapter 8	59
Chapter 9	68
Chapter 10	78
Chapter 11	86
Chapter 12	95
Chapter 13	103
Chapter 14	113
Chapter 15	123
Chapter 16	134
Chapter 17	142
Chapter 18	149
Chapter 19	158
Chapter 20	166
Chapter 21	174
Chapter 22	181
Chapter 23	188
Chapter 24	194
Chapter 25	202
Chapter 26	211
Chapter 27	221
Chapter 28	229
Epilogue	238
The Clue of the Brilliant Bastard - Chapter One	245
Also by Ellie St. Clair	255
About the Author	259

♥ **Copyright 2022 Ellie St Clair**

All rights reserved.

This book or parts thereof may not be reproduced in any form, stored in any retrieval system, or transmitted in any form by any means—electronic, mechanical, photocopy, recording, or otherwise—without prior written permission of the publisher.

Facebook: Ellie St. Clair

Cover by AJF Designs

Do you love historical romance? Receive access to a free ebook, as well as exclusive content such as giveaways, contests, freebies and advance notice of pre-orders through my mailing list!

Sign up here!

The Remingtons
The Mystery of the Debonair Duke
The Secret of the Dashing Detective
The Clue of the Brilliant Bastard
The Quest of the Reclusive Rogue

For a full list of all of Ellie's books, please see
www.elliestclair.com/books.

CHAPTER 1

"You may call it a prison, but it is certainly the loveliest prison I have ever seen."

Juliana couldn't help but laugh at her dearest friend and now sister-in-law. Emma always found a way to see the light in most situations, no matter how dire they might be.

"I suppose I am being rather dramatic," Juliana admitted, tapping her fingertips against the stone bench beneath her. "I am well aware that most people would give anything to be trapped in one of London's finest mansions."

"You are correct," Emma said diplomatically as she dug a hole in the garden bed next to Juliana's bench before pouring water into it from the pot at her side. "And yet, I understand that feeling trapped is feeling trapped, no matter what luxuries might surround you."

Juliana sighed. "You do understand me as no one else does."

Her sister, Prudence, snorted from the path she was walking on around the circular flower bed, close enough that she could remain part of the conversation. "I am right here, Jules."

Juliana rolled her eyes good-naturedly with a smile for her elder sister.

"You know I love you as much as I love anyone, Pru, but we will never completely understand one another."

"I suppose that is true."

Juliana allowed her eyes to drift over the great expanse of gardens that composed the grounds surrounding Warwick House. It sat a few streets east of Berkley Square in the middle of London. At one point in time, it had been near the edge of the city, but was now ringed by houses, businesses and neighbourhoods. Yet it still felt like one could become lost in here, away from the crowds of most London streets.

It could also feel rather isolating.

"Giles is only trying to keep you safe, Juliana," Emma said softly.

"I know," Juliana replied. It was true – her brother *was* trying to keep her safe. Their family was clearly under threat. They had thought their father's death over a year ago had been an isolated incident, even though the physician had told them he had likely been poisoned. It was widely assumed that Juliana's brother had killed him due to the hatred between him and their father, but no one had yet legally questioned the new duke.

Just over a month ago, however, Juliana had been abducted as the kidnappers intended to draw out Giles, to kill him too – and the plan had nearly worked. Fortunately, Giles had only been grazed by the bullet.

"Here we thought we would be done with all of this after Mr. Archibald found the man that kidnapped you," Prudence said, drawing Emma's ire when she snapped a flower off a bush and began to pick the petals off one at a time. Juliana knew she would be chanting the "loves me not" rhyme, even though Prudence didn't have potential suitors – nor, apparently, did she wish for any.

"We should have known it would be much more complicated than that," Emma murmured as she gently picked up a small sapling and placed it in the hole before pushing dirt around it.

"I shall never understand why a duchess sits in the dirt and works with the plants herself," Prudence said, her nose wrinkling as she watched Emma, who simply laughed at her.

"First, I only became a duchess two weeks ago, and I enjoyed such work long before that," Emma said. "Secondly, there is nothing that fills my soul like sitting in the gardens or the orangery and working with plants. You should try it."

"No, thank you," Prudence said politely as she continued her slow stroll.

"Why, do you have too much else to do?" Juliana asked, raising an eyebrow, and Prudence eyed her with a withering glare.

"Who are you to be asking me such a thing?"

"I have much to do," Juliana said indignantly, sitting up straight on the bench now. "My work is important."

Prudence clasped her hands behind her back.

"I know it was important to you, Jules, but Giles will never allow you to go back."

Juliana stared at her mutinously. "We shall see about that."

"Perhaps once we have this threat negated," Emma began diplomatically, but Juliana stopped her words with a wave of her hand.

"You are married to my brother now, Emma, which is wonderful and I am so happy we are now sisters and actually live together, but really, how would you like being kept under lock and key and told where you can go and who you can see?"

"You do not have to remain here," Emma said, moving

onto the next hole. "You are welcome to leave, which means that you are not a true prisoner."

"I can leave, but only if I am accompanied by Mr. Archibald."

"Yes," Emma conceded, rising to her feet and brushing dirt off the knees of the morning gown she had ruined long ago but kept for activities such as these. "He is not so horrible, though, now is he? Rather pleasant to look at, I believe you said at one point in time."

"He will report everything to Giles," Juliana grumbled, crossing her arms over her chest. Her brother had initially hired Matthew Archibald to determine who had killed their father – or to at least make it appear that he was trying to come to some conclusion, for at the time, Giles could have cared less who had taken their father out of this world. When Juliana had been abducted, however, Mr. Archibald had helped the family to recover her. Since then, the detective had been attempting to determine who was behind the scheme while also keeping the family safe.

"It is not as though you do anything disreputable," Prudence added in.

"No." Juliana took off her bonnet and set it next to her as she raised her face to the sun, waving away Prudence's warning regarding her freckles. "But there are some activities I take part in that Giles wouldn't exactly be… pleased about."

"Activities that he has forbidden?" Emma asked, looking over at her now, and Juliana heaved a dramatic sigh.

"It doesn't make any sense whatsoever, Emma. Even you must admit that. Mrs. Stone is a lovely woman and there is no reason to keep me from my work. We are not harming anyone. In fact, we are doing the exact opposite."

"I think it is more so that he is worried about what might

happen to you if you continue to take a stand for what you believe in."

"You sound like my mother now," Juliana said, chewing on her thumbnail.

"Oh, Jules, I am sorry," Emma said, walking over to her now. She lifted a hand to place it on Juliana's arm but stopped when they both looked down and saw how dirty it was. "You know I love you more than anything."

"I do," Juliana said with a nod and a smile, for she knew what Emma said was true.

"Good," Emma said, relief evident on her face. Their friendship hadn't been quite as strong and sure since Emma and Giles had married. "Now, do tell us, how is everything with Lord Hemingway?"

"Lord Hemingway?" Juliana asked with some surprise. She hadn't even considered the man as they sat in the afternoon sun, for she had been intent on how to return to her work despite Giles having forbidden it. "He is…" She tried to think of the right words to describe the man her mother was encouraging her to accept. "He is my father's cousin's son."

"Obviously," Prudence said with a snort.

"And he is…"

Juliana scratched her nose.

"Boring?" Prudence supplied, and Juliana opened her mouth to refute her, but found it impossible to do so directly.

"He is nice."

"Nice?" Prudence repeated. "Nice is what you use to describe something that you have nothing bad to say about but nothing particularly good either."

"I do not know him well," Juliana said defensively. "He has visited with us before, of course, when he has accompanied his mother, and he did call upon us in order to request a potential courtship, but we have not yet had the opportunity to spend much time together."

"How interesting it would be with Mr. Archibald following you around," Emma said, unable to hold back her laughter, to which Juliana could only sigh, wondering what that would look like.

The truth – one that she hadn't shared even with Emma – was that Prudence was right. Lord Hemingway was rather boring, even if he was everything she had thought she had wanted – a man she could tolerate, who would allow her to live the life she chose. At least, she assumed he would. He didn't exactly seem to be a man of strong opinions, not with a mother like his. But she also wasn't entirely sure she was prepared for anything unpredictable. Not any more. She'd had enough surprises already, and her other secret was just how much her abduction had affected her. Boring and predictable? She didn't have much issue with that at the moment.

"Now," Emma said, "the question is, how are you going to handle Mr. Archibald?"

* * *

MATTHEW ARCHIBALD DRUMMED his fingers on the desk in front of him, leaning back as he surveyed the room. His offices were small, located in the front of a tall brick building in the midst of Holborn. It was a respectable enough location that his higher-class clients felt comfortable in meeting him here, while it wasn't so high up that those who hired him from his own social status were not too intimidated to seek him out.

At the moment, the room in front of him was filled with the men who worked for him, the ones he could trust implicitly. He was currently failing at the most important job he had ever acquired, and he needed all of the help he could get.

The men were at ease, some sitting on the chairs they had

gathered from various corners of the room, some on the other desks that were available for use when needed. Still others were leaning against the wall, in relaxed poses. Matthew couldn't help a small smile for those he had gathered. They were good men, hard-working, reliable.

And he was letting them down.

He cleared his throat to capture their attention, and the ten men in the room immediately quieted down and turned to him.

Matthew inclined his head, signaling one man to come to the front with him. Owen Green had not only been his closest of friends since they were boys, but he had been the one to begin this operation with him all those years ago, and he had remained by his side ever since. On the days Matthew wished he had two of himself, Owen became that second person for him.

"Listen up, men," he said, as shocked as he had always been at how many now worked for him. Theirs had been a slow build to their current size, but he appreciated the trust of each and every one of them. "You know that we have had some difficulty in watching over the duke and his family. After Lady Juliana's abduction, we vowed to keep the family safe, and yet someone was able to enter their premises at the country house just outside Watford. We returned to London as it would be easier to watch over them all at Warwick House. It is, of course, large itself, but not nearly as sprawling as Remington House in the country."

They were all watching him, heads nodding. None of this was news, and they had all taken their turns guarding the houses and the family.

"Thus far, we have kept them safe here in London. That is because of you, and I thank you for that. But it is more important than ever for us to determine who is threatening them so that we can finish this job. The duke will not continue to pay us forever."

He saw some glances of unease between the men. Up until now, most of their jobs had come to a fairly swift conclusion. But then, most were not particularly complicated. A husband getting cuckolded, a theft that was so obvious that Matthew wondered how the victim couldn't have determined the culprit himself.

"What you do not know is that we have uncovered a secret from the previous duke's past. He had an illegitimate son with a woman by the name of Mrs. Lewis. She used to live in the village near the duke's country seat but moved to London some years ago, likely to accompany her son when he came to school here. The duke had been paying her – perhaps blackmail? – until about five years ago. We have located the son and I am going to make contact with him to determine what he knows and what ill will he could hold toward the family."

"How will you do that?" one man, Pip, asked from the back.

"I'm going to establish a friendship," Matthew said. "It will be much easier to draw him out that way than attempt to force information out of him."

Much more palatable, that was. He had tried both ways before and always struggled with the latter.

"Do we have any other suspects?" another man, Anderson, asked him now, and Matthew tapped his fingers on the desk again as he let Owen answer, for he had been the one keeping an eye on the other suspect.

"We cannot forget about Lord Hemingway, simply because he is the one who would gain the title if anything were to happen to the duke," Owen said. "But the man is as clean as they come. Has never even cheated at gambling from what I can tell. No one has a bad word to say about him. He's just a good man, if a bit under his mother's thumb. He is interested in courting the Lady Juliana, so he will remain part of the family, if nothing else."

"Keep an eye on him, just in case," Matthew said, wondering why he felt that instinctual turn of his stomach when Owen spoke of Hemingway's interest in Lady Juliana. What did it matter to him if the two got together?

"I will."

"While I attempt to befriend Lewis, I will not be able to watch him at other times, for the duke has requested that I remain available to ensure Lady Juliana's safety," Matthew continued. "She received a threatening note when out at the museum not long ago, and the duke is concerned that she has been targeted as the weakest point in the family. So Mouse, you will also watch over Lewis, see what else he is up to. Good?"

"Good."

"The rest of you will continue your shifts watching over the family as we have discussed. Then we have the few of you who are on the Sheffield case."

He moved the discussion over to the smaller case, while his mind remained on the Warwick threat. He was missing something, he knew it. He rubbed his chin as a piece of information poked at the back of his mind but didn't quite make it through.

Just what was it?

CHAPTER 2

*J*uliana was restless. She tapped her toe on the pink, white, and gold patterned Aubusson carpet below her as she stabbed the canvas in her hands with more passion than anyone had likely ever used in needlepoint before.

"Are you all right?" Prudence asked from her place across the room.

"Fine," Juliana muttered.

"You don't seem fine," Prudence said matter-of-factly. "You are mutilating your needlepoint."

"Well, then, it will not look much different than it usually does."

Prudence smiled but continued to read her book.

Juliana threw down the needlepoint in frustration. "I need to go somewhere. Do something. I cannot sit here and make meaningless holes in a canvas for a minute longer."

"It is not as though today has been anything out of the ordinary," Prudence remarked. "It is just that you are not allowed to leave, is that not it?"

"It is," Juliana sighed. "I feel stifled."

"Why do you not plan an outing, then?" Prudence asked. "You simply need to arrange it with Mr. Archibald."

"I suppose," Juliana mused. "But then he might tell Giles where I would like to go, and that would never do."

"I do not suppose it would," Prudence said with a knowing smile as she was well aware of just where that was on Juliana's mind.

"What time is it?" Juliana asked, sitting up suddenly.

"Eleven o'clock."

"I must go outside to the gardens."

"To feed your strays?"

"Yes, as a matter of fact," Juliana said. She was nearly out the door when Prudence called to her once more.

"Does it bother you?" Prudence asked.

"Does what bother me?" Juliana asked. What more could Prudence want to know about her imprisonment?

"Giles and Emma."

"Giles and Emma? Of course not," she said, waving a hand in the air. "I am as happy for them as I could be for any two people."

Which was partially true. She was overjoyed that her brother and her closest friend were happy. Emma was her sister in truth now. It was just... odd. And she wondered how her own relationship with Emma was going to change now that Emma was the duchess and the woman of the house. They had moments where everything seemed as it had been before but there were many others when they were reminded of their new situation.

"I suppose it is just in how the way our lives have changed... I cannot trust Emma like I once did. I do not know whether her allegiance is to me or to Giles."

"Perhaps it is to both of you."

"Perhaps. But I cannot be sure."

"I understand," Prudence said, nodding wisely. "You can always talk to me, Jules. You know that, do you not?"

"I do," Juliana said with a smile as Prudence placed a mark in her book and set it on the table. "Where are you going?"

"To the fencing room," Prudence replied, standing and straightening her skirts.

"I should join you."

"You should. You should learn how to defend yourself, what with all the threats on your life."

Juliana bit her lip. Prudence was right. And perhaps if it had been Prudence who had been abducted, she wouldn't have had to wait for someone else to come save her, for she would have saved herself. But it was too late for regrets. Besides, there was someone awaiting her now.

"I shall see you at dinner," she said. Her first task would be finding the butler, Jameson, to arrange for Mr. Archibald to accompany her on a task, before she made her way down to the kitchens.

She greeted their cook, Chamberlain, who already had a bowl of scraps waiting for her. It was the only time Juliana ever touched meat, refusing to eat any of it herself. But she could hardly subject her strays to tops of carrots and potato peels, not when they were accustomed to an entirely different diet.

"Give them a pet for me, will you, my lady?" Chamberlain asked, and Juliana nodded as her spirit lifted somewhat when she took the servants' staircase up and stepped out into the sun, which, for once in London's late spring this year, was shining gloriously.

By the time she made it to the back wall of the grounds, she could see them waiting for her, lined up by the iron fence. It always amazed her how animals seemed to be able to tell time instinctually. The truth was, she found a kinship

THE SECRET OF THE DASHING DETECTIVE

with her animals much more than she did nearly any person outside of Emma.

"Here we are," she said as the dogs and two cats who were brave enough to accompany them took their turns awaiting her gifts. She considered how far they had come. When she had first started feeding them, they would practically attack one another for her offerings, but over time they had come to understand that there would be enough for all of them – she always made sure of it.

And there at the end was the little dog, the one that she called Lucy.

"Good morning, lovely," she said, reaching through the iron bars and scratching the small dog's head. One of her ears had been battered long ago, and she had taken the longest to warm up to Juliana. After a great deal of affection and scraps of meat, she now leaned into Juliana's hand with devotion.

Juliana sat there in the sun, soaking up her time here, wishing that she could take some of them home with her. But of course, her mother had forbidden it the one time she had tried long ago, and Giles also hadn't been particularly keen on the idea.

If she married Lord Hemingway, would he allow her to take them in?

She pursed her lips, unsure why that thought caused such discord to run through her belly. For if he did, it would all be worth it – wouldn't it?

* * *

HOLBORN WASN'T the worst neighbourhood. It was not St. Giles or Covent Garden, that was for certain. And yet, Matthew's short journey to Mayfair certainly showcased the stark contrast between where he was coming from to where he was going. He had lived his entire life in London, and yet when his work had taken him to the country, he had realized how much London left to be desired.

Mayfair, however, was like stepping into another world, one in which he would never belong. It was beautiful, of course, with the symmetrical rows of townhouses around beautiful green squares and the tall, clean brick buildings housing establishments where only the elite were invited. And there, on the edge, was the majesty of Warwick House. Matthew imagined that his entire neighbourhood could fit into the grounds, and there would still be room for more.

He shook his head as he climbed the stairs and knocked on the door. His was an interesting position. He was not a servant, but he was a hired man. Yet, the duke had been clear that he was to use the front entrance, which Matthew appreciated. The man had always treated him with respect – even when Matthew and his men had failed to uphold their responsibility.

"Jameson," Matthew greeted the butler, who nodded a return greeting to him. "I have been summoned by the Lady Juliana."

"Yes, she would like to go out."

"Very well. Is she ready?"

Jameson shook her head. "I believe she will be some time."

Matthew tried to tamp down his impatience. He was being paid for this, he reminded himself, and yet he knew this was just the beginning of what would be the spoiled princess act that he had expected.

"Has she gone somewhere?"

He could ask that, he supposed, as it was his job to follow her and keep her safe.

"She is out on the grounds."

"Alone?" Matthew raised his eyebrows, but then, it wasn't

THE SECRET OF THE DASHING DETECTIVE

Jameson's fault. The man was not Lady Juliana's keeper. Matthew was – for the moment, at least.

"I am not entirely sure who has accompanied her today. You are likely to find her at the northwest corner if you are inclined to seek her out."

"Thank you, Jameson," Matthew said, returning the way he had come. At least the weather was fine today. He could use more time outdoors. He walked around the property, musing, as he always did, at how all of this could belong to one man, one family – and that this was only one of their many homes.

He also realized as he walked just how easy it would be for someone to enter the grounds and find one of the family members here. What was Lady Juliana thinking, wandering the gardens alone? Had the woman no sense of self-preservation? Not only that, he thought selfishly, but if something were to happen to her, his own business would be ruined, even if her downfall was the result of her own stupidity.

He finally spotted the splash of blue, crouched down at the corner of the iron fence. A bonnet covered her head, but he could picture her chestnut hair beneath it. He may be dreading this assignment, but he couldn't deny her attractiveness, that was for certain.

Lady Juliana was reaching for something, her hand through the bars. What on earth was she doing? He squinted as he tried to see what was on the other side of the fence. He saw a shape move and wondered if it could be a person. Begging? Asking her for help? Convincing her to come out? He continued to walk closer, his speed increasing as he felt the need to reach her quickly in case she was in danger.

When he neared, he finally saw what was on the other side of the fence and he stopped in surprise.

"Lady Juliana?" he called, and she yelped, falling back out of her crouch and landing on her bottom.

The dogs on the other side of the fence responded to his presence and her cry by turning and running away – except for one, who stood there and eyed him, as if trying to determine whether or not to trust him with the woman who cared for them. Finally, with one small bark, the mangy thing turned and ran after the others.

Matthew strode over to the duke's sister, currently sitting on the ground rather dejectedly until he stood next to her and she glared up at him. He reached out a hand to help her up. She eyed it like it was dirty.

"Come on," he said. "Stand up."

She let out a sound that seemed to be part snarl as she finally took his hand and stood. Her bare hand was soft in his, warm and... was it sticky?

"I don't suppose you want to tell me what you are doing out here?" he said, raising an eyebrow.

"I do not suppose I do," she said, lifting her chin, and he had to rein in a sigh. Her brother had warned him that she was not pleased with having someone watch over her every move, but it annoyed him that she couldn't see the reason for it all.

"You know we are on the same side here," he said, and she shook her head, taking a step back away from him.

"Incorrect. You are on my brother's side."

"He has hired me, yes. But I am here to keep you safe. You do not want a repeat of what happened to you before, do you?"

Her eyes shifted to the side for a moment, in a motion that was the only sign she was, perhaps, more affected by the situation than she had originally let on. "No."

"Then we will work together. What were you doing with those dogs?"

"Feeding them."

"They are stray mongrels."

"They are."

"Why would the sister of a duke feed stray dogs?"

"Why would she not?" she countered, and Matthew had to hold back a smile at her spunk.

"Very well, then," he said. "Feed your dogs. But you cannot come out here alone. We always have men here, guarding the house. Take one of them with you if I am not here."

"I do not want to bother them for this."

"It is our job," he said, in some frustration.

"But I – very well," she finally said, raising her hands in the air in defeat.

"I startled you when I came upon you, and you sat on the ground helplessly," he said, knowing that he was going to draw out her anger, but perhaps that is what she needed. "What would you have done if I were here to harm you?"

She opened her mouth, but no sound came out, and he knew that he had her there.

"Strike me," he said, and her eyebrows lifted beneath her pristine white bonnet.

"Pardon me?"

"Strike me. Show me what you would do if I was here to take you again."

"I—"

"You are helpless. Why are they targeting you, and not your sister, or the duke's wife, your friend? There must be a reason."

Her brows furrowed now as her lips pursed, and he knew he was drawing her out.

"Strike me," he said again.

"No."

"Do it."

"I—"

"Or are you too weak?"

That seemed to convince her. Her hand drew back and her arm moved forward, in an obvious attempt to slap him across the face. He caught her wrist just before she made contact.

"What am I, a woman who has slighted you? A slap across the face will do nothing but insult me."

"You do know that I am a lady, do you not?"

"I do, but I don't particularly care when it comes to your safety," he countered. "Now, make a fist."

She reluctantly did as he said, her fingers curling around her thumb.

"Not like that," he said, reaching out and rearranging her thumb in front of her knuckles. "Like this. Now, turn your fist as you direct it toward me so you hit me with the knuckles of your hand."

He braced himself for the impact, as slight as it might be.

"Where?" she asked in some bewilderment.

"Here," he said, pointing to a place just beneath his breastbone.

"Very well," she said, and then stepped back and brought her fist forward with all of her might.

Matthew had to work to contain his slight grunt.

"Good," he said. "We'll work on it, along with a few other things."

"Such as?" she asked, some intrigue sparking in her eyes.

"You are interested now?"

"I am interested in not being a victim again," she said, her jaw setting in determination. "If you are able to help with that, then I will take it."

Matthew grinned. Perhaps this was going to be more entertaining than he had first imagined.

CHAPTER 3

This was more than likely a very bad idea. And yet Juliana couldn't help the slight thrill that ran through her at the prospect of, for once, being able to protect herself.

Even if she had to learn from Matthew Archibald.

"How were you taken last time?"

Juliana swallowed. She always tried not to think of that event. Her abduction had been the most horrible two days of her life, even though she knew she had been lucky that nothing worse had happened to her than being hungry and tired and panicky at the thought she might never escape.

"A hood was put over my head, and arms wrapped around me from behind," she said, unable to look at Mr. Archibald as she said it, for she didn't want him to see how affected she was.

"What did you do?"

"I tried to kick backward, but he held me too far away from his body to do anything. His hand was over my mouth so I couldn't even scream."

Mr. Archibald nodded. "That makes sense. I will tell you

what do if it ever happens again – not that it will, as I should always be with you. But it is good to be prepared."

"Very well," she said, swallowing hard at the thought of another threat.

"Drop your body weight – go limp," he said. "Then, if you are able to, step on his foot with all of your might. If you can't reach it, try to grab his fingers – the index and middle finger of each hand, and pull as hard as you can. If you cannot reach his hands, try to dig your elbows into his abdomen, or if you can get a hand up, pull on his ear. There are options, depending on what is available to you in that moment. Use all the strength that you have."

She nodded, trying to process it all. "That is a lot to remember."

"Learning is best done by doing," he said. "Come away from the fence, and we will practice."

He led her deeper behind the hedgerows and then stepped behind her and wrapped his arms around her. She stiffened in memory of the last time someone had done this, but he murmured in her ear, "It's just me. You're safe."

She nodded, surprised at how comfortable she did feel in his grip. If nothing else, she knew that he was a man of his word and was skilled at what he did.

"Now," he said. "What are you able to do?"

She tried going limp in his arms, but nothing happened – he was too strong. She remembered his words and reached for his hands. He anticipated her move and wrapped his arms tighter around her. In doing so, she realized he was focused on her arm movements, and she lifted her leg and stomped down on his boot as hard as she could.

"Good," he said. "Now I'm distracted, so try digging your elbows into my abdomen."

She did, and his grip slightly loosened.

"Now turn," he instructed, and when she did, she found

THE SECRET OF THE DASHING DETECTIVE

she had enough space to face him. "Remember that punch?" he asked, and she nodded.

"You do the same punch, but right here," he pointed to his throat. "And then you run like hell."

She knew her eyes widened somewhat. Most men would never speak like that in her presence. But then, he was not most men.

"I can do that," she said, and he eyed her with a challenge.

"Say that with more confidence," he directed.

"I can *do* that," she said, and for the first time today, she took a good look at him. He dressed well, although not nearly as fine as Giles, of course, which she supposed made sense, for his work was far different from what Giles was used to every day. His shoulders were broad, his muscles apparent even beneath the fine cut of his clothes.

His sandy hair was uncovered, his tanned face upturned to the sun. He wasn't handsome in the traditional sense of most men of her acquaintance with his Romanesque nose slightly hooked to one side, but with his sculpted cheekbones, he was... striking and much more attractive, in a way. He was a man who could take care of a woman.

She was startled when she realized that her pulse was beating faster than usual, which must be from her exertions. For a man like him shouldn't have her feeling anything out of the ordinary.

"We'll practice another time," he said, "but we should return. You had somewhere you would like to go?"

"Oh, yes," she said. "But I must ask you something first."

"Very well," he said, as they began walking back to the house. Juliana had a strange desire to take his arm, but as he didn't offer it, she of course didn't make any motion to do so.

"Would you tell Giles where we went?"

He said nothing for a moment, and Juliana snuck a glance

at him. He seemed to be providing much thought to her question.

"I suppose if he asked me, I would feel compelled to tell him," he said, looking back toward her. "Is that satisfactory?"

"No," she sighed. "But it might have to do. I have a meeting later."

"A meeting?" he seemed suspicious, which she understood. Most sisters of dukes would not have business to partake in.

"Yes," she said. "In Holborn."

"I see."

"I would prefer that Giles not know about it."

"Is there any reason to suspect that you might be in danger?"

"None whatsoever," she said with as much confidence as she could muster. And there wasn't – for her society had not yet started any activities that would draw attention to them. When they did, well, that might be another situation entirely but she saw no need to concern Matthew Archibald with that right now.

"What time is it at?"

"Three o'clock. The meetings used to be in the evenings, but now that Giles has Emma, he is much less likely to go out to his clubs, and I suppose it is safer for me to be out of the house in the day rather than the evening. Luckily, the rest of the attendees have accommodated me, despite their own schedules."

"You are the sister of a duke. I am sure most of the members of this mysterious meeting in Holborn are quite pleased to have you in their presence."

"I am no different from the rest of them. In our endeavors, we are all equals," she said, waving away his words, not liking to be reminded that she might be seen as different

THE SECRET OF THE DASHING DETECTIVE

from the others. "Now, speaking of mystery, tell me about yourself."

He turned to her with one eyebrow raised. "You want to know about me?"

"If we are to be spending so much time together, whyever not?"

"I am working for your family. We are not acquaintances."

Juliana pursed her lips at the obstinate man. She was intrigued by him, that much she could admit to herself. He was so different from any other man of her acquaintance. He was a detective, yet he seemed to know how to fit in with the upper class when required. She glanced down and caught a look at his hands, remembering what they had felt like when they had helped her from the ground – strong, slightly roughened, nothing at all like the men she was used to.

"How did you become a detective?"

"My father was a constable with Bow Street. I followed his line of work."

"Why do you not work for Bow Street as well?"

"I prefer to work for myself rather than for someone else."

"You are working for my brother now."

His nostrils flared slightly, and Juliana wondered if she was annoying him. "That's different," was all he said. "He is a client."

"Very well," she continued. "Are you from London?"

"Yes?"

"Whereabouts were you raised?"

"Holborn."

"Oh, that is where Mrs. Stone lives!" When he eyed her, she added, "the woman we will be visiting later today."

"I see."

She could sense his growing frustration as they neared the house, although she had no idea what she had done to cause such ire.

"Have I offended you in some way?" she asked, stopping at the edge of the stairs leading up to the terrace.

"No. Why would you think that?"

"Finding answers from you is like pulling out the stubborn weeds in Emma's gardens."

He smiled slightly at that, and she was glad to see that there was some humor within him.

"There is nothing intriguing about me, Lady Juliana. I am simply a man, hired to do a job. I see no reason why my background would be of any interest to you."

"Every person is of interest, Mr. Archibald."

"I disagree."

She started up the stairs. "I do not much care for having a guard, Mr. Archibald, but I would be amenable to a friend."

"I would assume you have many friends already," he countered, following her up.

"Not many of the human variety," she said, a faint smile on her lips as she enjoyed the back-and-forth banter with him.

Juliana pushed through the garden doors which led into the ballroom, and it took her a few steps to realize that Mr. Archibald was no longer following her. She turned to find that he had stopped just in the entryway, his eyes studying the room. She followed his gaze, trying to see it through a stranger's view. Greek gods and goddesses flew and danced across the ceiling, while painted ivy wrapped around the tops of the marble pillars. It was quite extravagant, especially since they so rarely used the room, although she was sure that was going to change now that Juliana's father had passed and they were out of mourning. They had already hosted one successful ball – the very one when Emma and Giles had first determined an interest in one another.

"It is quite a room, isn't it?" she asked, to which he nodded but said nothing.

THE SECRET OF THE DASHING DETECTIVE

He followed her in silence through the ballroom until they came to the doors leading out to the drawing room beyond.

Where her mother was waiting.

"Juliana," she said, a smile crossing her face. "I was looking for you."

"Oh?" she said, coming to a stop so quickly that she felt Mr. Archibald nearly run into her, although he stopped himself in time.

"Yes," she said, her satisfied expression worrying Juliana, for it meant that she was up to something. "Lord Hemingway and his mother will be here shortly. You best get dressed. You can hardly greet them in that gown."

She cast her gaze up and down Juliana's now-soiled morning dress.

She could only look at her mother with unease as she tried to think of how to get out the day's engagement. She could hardly tell her where she had planned to go.

"You didn't tell me they were coming."

"No, but it is not as though you have anywhere else to be."

"Actually, I do," Juliana said as her mind desperately raced for an excuse she could present without providing the truth.

"Which would be?" her mother said, waiting.

"I—I must visit Lady Maria!" she burst out, wondering where that had come from. She barely knew Lady Maria, the woman her mother had been hoping her brother would marry before he became interested in Emma.

Her mother was not currently convinced.

"Lady Maria Bennington?"

"Yes," Juliana forged on, as it was too late to back away now. "We became… friendly when she and her mother visited us in the country. I told her I would call upon her today."

Her mother considered this information for a moment before pursing her lips.

"Very well. We shall have a quick tea with Lord and Lady Hemingway and then we will go visit Lady Maria and Lady Bennington."

"Oh, no," Juliana said desperately. "Lady Maria's mother is... out."

"Out?"

"Yes, she is out for the day. That is why Lady Maria asked that I visit this afternoon. To provide her company."

"Very well," her mother said, waving her hand. "Please do change quickly. It would never do for Lord Hemingway to see you like that."

Juliana began to take a step toward the staircase, forgetting Mr. Archibald's presence until she ran into him, but he smoothly backed up.

"Juliana?" her mother said before she could leave the room.

"Yes."

"I know Mr. Archibald is here to ensure your safety, but it would be best for the two of you not to be alone – even out of doors. Do you understand me?"

She addressed Juliana, but she saw her mother's eyes were not on her, but on Mr. Archibald behind her, and Juliana had to swallow her embarrassment. She opened her mouth to retort, but finally decided that Mr. Archibald would be fine to manage this situation. Sometimes the best course of action was simply to run away.

CHAPTER 4

Matthew heard the dowager duchess' comments loud and clear. *Stay away from my daughter*.

Which was all well and good except that he had been hired to follow her around.

It did, however, diminish the slight fire that had begun to spark at their conversation. For the truth was, as much as Lady Juliana's constant questioning slightly annoyed him, he was also intrigued by her, enjoyed her energy and spirit.

Not that it mattered.

For, as the dowager duchess had pointed out as if he couldn't remember himself, Lady Juliana was the sister of a duke, a woman who was practically promised to marry an earl.

While he was a detective, a man of middle class who had been hired by the family, just a slight step above a servant. It was as he had originally determined – he should not be conversing with the Lady Juliana, but instead walking a step behind her to see she came to no harm, as was required of him.

Now, with this change in plans, he was going to have to sit at Warwick House for an indeterminate amount of time while she chattered on with Hemingway. At least it could provide him with the opportunity to learn more about the man and whether he might have any actual inclination to do away with the duke. He seemed harmless, but he was next in line for the title, so he had more motive than any other. Matthew hadn't discussed this theory with the Duke of Warwick yet, for he knew he was friends with the man who was as close to a cousin as he had.

But one could often learn much more by observing then entering into the conversation.

Matthew stayed as unobtrusive as possible as Lord Hemingway and his mother arrived, greeting Lady Juliana and the dowager duchess. Lady Emma, or should he say now, the Duchess of Warwick, and Lady Prudence were, interestingly, nowhere to be found, which he supposed the dowager duchess had arranged for.

The visit, however, provided him with no additional clues as to whether Lord Hemingway was hiding anything. He was as cordial as ever, polite, said all the right things at the right time, and Matthew found himself having a difficult time picturing him killing a spider let alone taking a shot at the duke.

In fact, when the duke realized his cousin was in attendance and stopped in the entrance of the room, he seemed particularly pleased to see Hemingway. He had a nod for Matthew before he was on his way.

"Lurking, are we?"

Matthew jumped at the voice in his ear, coming from behind him. He wasn't typically a man who was caught unaware, but it seemed a woman had gotten the best of him.

A woman, he soon realized, who, despite her age and her cane, moved as stealthily as any thief.

"Lady Winchester," he said, recognizing the duke's grandmother. "How are you today?"

They stepped away from the doorway so as not to disturb anyone within.

"I am well," she said, studying him up and down. "Have you finished your job yet?"

Matthew was as disappointed in himself as the countess seemed to be in him at the moment.

"Not yet, I'm afraid," he said. "Although I hope that we should come to a swift conclusion soon."

She studied him through eyes that he recognized – eyes he realized were near identical to Lady Juliana's green ones, although Lady Winchester's were much wiser with age and slightly more clouded.

"Juliana wears a brave mask, but she is struggling with this," she said, surprising Matthew, for he had thought he was the only one to see that Lady Juliana had been more affected than she let on by the circumstances.

"Oh?" was all he said.

"You've seen it, my boy, I know you have," she said. "You're a smart one. You've got to be, to make a go out of your business. She needs watching, yes, but in more ways than you might think."

And with that cryptic line, she continued down the hallway, cane tapping, no longer as surreptitious as she had been when she had snuck up on him. Matthew smiled after her. She was an interesting woman, that was for certain, and he could see a lot of Lady Juliana in her.

Lady Juliana – who, when he took a glimpse into the drawing room, was no longer keeping any of her attention on the conversation, but rather was looking from the mantel clock to the doorway and back again. She caught his eye and sent him a silent plea that he could have sworn said, 'help me!' but who was he to come between social engagements of the noble set?

Finally, the tea broke up and he waited as Lady Juliana prepared herself to leave. This time, her maid, Abigail, accompanied them. The dowager duchess made sure of it.

Reminded of his place, Matthew sat up top of the carriage with the driver, while the maid sat within. The driver waited for a moment and Juliana surprised him when she leaned her head out of the window and said in a low hiss, "James, we are going to Mrs. Stone's."

"Very good, my lady," the driver said, before flicking the reins and sending the horses down the road.

Matthew looked over at the driver – James, Juliana had called him.

"What is waiting for us at Mrs. Stone's?"

"A gathering."

Matthew had an inkling of what it must be like to ask him questions.

"Who will be at this gathering?"

"A gathering of people who attend Lady Juliana's meetings."

Matthew took a breath.

"Meetings about what?"

The driver looked at him as though surprised he didn't know more. "Why, of Lady Juliana's society of course."

"Of course," Matthew muttered, realizing that he was likely going to have to learn for himself what this mysterious meeting was all about.

Soon enough the streets and houses changed into the familiar neighborhood where he had grown up and even now resided, although he wasn't going to share that information with Lady Juliana nor James nor anyone else. He had to keep this strictly professional, he reminded himself, even though his body couldn't help remembering what it had felt like to hold Lady Juliana in his arms as he had taught her how to protect herself. She was soft and warm and everything a man could ask for in a woman

But she was not the kind of woman he would ever know, he reminded himself.

The carriage came to a stop in front of a small red brick townhouse, one which looked quite tidy and well-kept. Matthew disembarked and held out a hand for Lady Juliana, who took it with a small smile before walking up to the house.

The maid followed, and Matthew was close behind her.

"You do not need to accompany me inside, Mr. Archibald," Lady Juliana said. "I can assure you that I am quite safe with everyone who is within."

"Be that as it may," he said firmly so that she would not argue any further, "I will wait inside, although I promise to be unobtrusive."

"Very well," she said with a shrug, turning back to him once more before knocking on the door. "Perhaps you might also learn a thing or two." She flashed him a quick, cheeky smile before turning back around, and he wondered what that might mean, but forgot it as the door opened to reveal a short woman with a wide, welcoming smile.

"Lady Juliana, I am so happy you are able to join us again," she said, reaching out and half-hugging her. "I was so worried after your brother—"

"All is well," Lady Juliana interrupted, and Matthew had a sinking feeling that he had been manipulated into taking Lady Juliana somewhere that Giles would not have approved of. All he could do now, however, was follow her in and see what came of this.

* * *

JULIANA WAS SLIGHTLY nervous as she took a seat on Mrs. Stone's pink floral sofa, which was pretty, if slightly worn. Juliana knew that Mr. Stone worked hard as a milliner, but their home, while lovely and comfortable, was a far cry from what she was used to. It made her feel rather guilty that she had so much while others had so little, but she was also aware that to try to make any offer would only affect the Stones' pride. And so she attended the meetings, leaving her privilege at the door, and participated as any other. That wasn't why she was here.

She took a deep breath in and out as she tried not to allow her nerves to overwhelm her. She had never been nervous at these meetings before, except perhaps her very first one. She had a feeling it was due to Mr. Archibald's presence, although why that would so bother her, she had no idea. He affected her in some way, although how or why, she couldn't be certain. He was just a man, a man who had been hired by her family. But she had already been embarrassed enough today by the scene he had witnessed when her mother had ambushed her with Lord Hemingway. Goodness, how little control could one person have over her own life?

And Lord Hemingway himself. She sighed. He was so pleasant that it was difficult to find any reason to say no to his suit or courtship. She thought of Emma, and knew exactly what her friend would tell her – to not settle unless she had found true love. Which was fine for Emma, whose true love had been standing in front of her nearly her entire life. Juliana, however, was already three and twenty, her come-out having been delayed by first her father and then her father's death, and she knew she didn't have much time to search for the passionate love Emma had always so desperately wanted. Not when she desired a certain life, one that included the ability to further her cause and be with someone who would allow her the freedom to do as she

THE SECRET OF THE DASHING DETECTIVE

pleased. If nothing else, Lord Hemingway would likely allow her to do so.

She fidgeted in her seat, stealing glances at Mr. Archibald, standing stoically against the wall, arms crossed over his chest. He had this uncanny ability to simply be. To stand there, doing nothing but observing.

Juliana could hardly imagine anything more unnerving. She always had to be doing something – if not moving, then in conversation. It was also why she hadn't yet given up her horrific needlework. It kept her hands busy.

"Good afternoon, everyone," Mrs. Stone said, as she stood before the armchair that was placed at the front of the room. "Thank you so much for coming."

Juliana smiled at everyone as they greeted one another. There was the poet, Mr. Smith. The surgeon and his wife, Mr. and Mrs. Livingstone. Another young woman about her age, Miss Polley, and a middle-aged couple, the vicar Father Abbot and his wife.

"Today we are here to discuss our next steps, including how we would like to spread our information, to encourage more people to join us and to make a difference. Does anyone have any suggestions?"

They all looked at one another around the room, before Juliana hesitantly stood up.

"I do have one."

"Of course," Mrs. Stone said with an encouraging smile.

"What if we were to create a pamphlet?" she asked, looking around at them all. "We have much expertise in this room. Mr. Livingstone could provide the medical information on how he has seen a natural vegetarian diet heal various ailments and provide general overall wellbeing. Father Abbott can perhaps provide us passages from the Bible for religious evidence to confirm our suppositions.

And Mr. Smith, I am sure you can write beautiful verses to accompany their words."

She smiled at them all as she spoke to each of them, and she could see how they glowed in the praise.

"The rest of us can work together on providing various viewpoints and amalgamating all of the information into prose that can help convince the public."

There were some nods around the room.

"That is all well and good, Lady Juliana," Miss Polley said, pushing her glasses up her nose as she crossed her hands in her lap. "But what of those who cannot read? Or who cannot afford to purchase such a product?"

"I am not suggesting that the pamphlet come at any cost," she said, shaking her head. "On the contrary, I believe it would be best to disseminate it for free so that more people are able to read it. Perhaps we could also provide some illustrations? I do not suppose anyone here is particularly artistic?"

They all shook their heads.

"Well, I suppose we would have to hire someone," she said, shrugging her shoulders. "But it is most certainly possible."

"That is a wonderful idea, Lady Juliana. Thank you," Mrs. Stone said.

"How would we afford this?" Mr. Smith asked, and Juliana wrung her hands together. She knew how it must look to the rest of them. Her family had more money than the rest of them combined many times over. And yet she had no ability to access nearly any of it.

She did, however, have a small allowance for clothing and small extravagances. Perhaps if she was able to save it for a time, she could pay for the printing. She certainly could not ask Giles for the money to do so.

"I shall fund it," she said with far more confidence than she felt.

"Are you certain?" Mrs. Stone asked, peering at her. "Please do not feel obligated to do so."

"Although it would hardly make a dent in her family's coffers," Mr. Smith added rather unhelpfully.

Juliana ignored him and smiled wide. "I would be happy to pay for it."

"Very well. That is settled, then," Mrs. Stone said, clapping her hands together. "Anyone else?"

"I have a question."

Juliana stilled. She knew that voice. She turned, her eyes wide at Mr. Archibald, who had stepped away slightly from the wall. The rest of the group began turning to one another murmuring about who he was and what he was doing there.

"Yes, Mr. Archibald?" Mrs. Stone said, for the two of them had been introduced at the door.

"Is such a publication likely to cause any issues? Potential danger to any of you? Is there anyone who would be disgruntled?"

They all paused for a moment, staring at him as though they hadn't considered a potential risk.

"There will be many who don't agree with such sentiments, that is for certain," Mrs. Stone said slowly. "But I can hardly imagine anyone becoming violent about such things. It is not as though the opinions of a group as small as ours would greatly affect anyone's way of life."

"It only takes one," he said, and Juliana tried to silently tell him with her glare not to say anything else at the moment, that instead they would discuss this afterward.

He did not take her hint.

CHAPTER 5

Matthew knew he had told Juliana that he was going to remain silent and simply observe.

He had been rather intrigued by the subject matter. He had never heard of anyone who objected to the practice of eating meat, and he couldn't quite understand it. But that didn't mean he wasn't slightly impressed by the fact that these people felt strongly enough about a cause to take a stand for it.

Lady Juliana spoke eloquently and decisively. He had seen a slight bit of unease on her face when she offered to print the pamphlet, and he supposed it was because as wealthy as her family was, she could hardly ask her brother for the funds for this. Not when he had, as Matthew now gathered, obviously been against Juliana's participation in such a society.

Knowing he was likely going to hear about this in the future from the duke, Matthew was most uneasy with Juliana's idea to begin sharing their opinions with society as a whole.

"What about those in the agricultural industry?" he

questioned. "Farmers? Those who run the markets at Smithfield? Might you be questioning their income, their way of life?"

The other young woman in the room bit her lip while Mrs. Stone's gaze hardened, as though she was preparing herself to fight for her cause no matter the consequences.

"I can understand your concern, Mr. Archibald," Mrs. Stone said, obviously trying to placate him. "Lady Juliana has the highest profile out of any of us and she could be targeted by anyone who would be upset, although my feeling is that the chances are rather low. Perhaps if the pamphlet does not mention any of our names? We could ask that anyone interested in joining us write to a separate address, and from there we can determine whether or not they are scrupulous enough to allow into our meetings."

Matthew considered the idea even as he ignored Lady Juliana's glare.

"Very well," he finally said. "You can provide my office address."

"Mr. Archibald," Lady Juliana said tersely, clearly controlling her ire with him, "I do not believe that is necessary. We do not require your involvement in this."

"I am happy to arrange it," he said. He then hesitated for a moment, for he hadn't had any intention to offer additional services, but at Lady Juliana's annoyance with him, he couldn't help teasing her more.

"I would also like to offer any drawings you require."

"Pardon me?" Lady Juliana said incredulously, an eyebrow lifted.

"I happen to have some artistic ability. You mentioned you need drawings. I would be happy to provide them."

Lady Juliana let out a sound that was half-cough, half-snort, and Matthew couldn't help a smile of satisfaction. He had no idea why, but he liked piquing this woman's temper.

"That would be wonderful, Mr. Archibald. Thank you," Mrs. Stone said with a warm smile.

"Mr. Archibald, are you a vegetarian?" Lady Juliana asked, even though she already knew the answer, piercing him with her green-eyed stare.

"I am not."

"Do you have any interest in seeing to the welfare of animals?"

"I suppose I do as much as anyone. I have no desire to see an animal in pain."

"But you do not fight against it, do you?" she pressed him.

"I have never before, but there is no time like the present." He smiled amiably, and Lady Juliana's frown deepened.

"It seems Mr. Archibald has been inspired by our meeting," Mrs. Stone said, apparently trying to ease the tension that had grown between Matthew and Lady Juliana. "Hopefully we can encourage others to join us and do the same."

The meeting continued as the group discussed other matters for the next hour. The conversation flowed from animal welfare to the latest books written on vegetarianism to recipes. Matthew found himself much more intrigued by this conversation than that which had taken place in the drawing room at Warwick House. It was interesting to see a group so diverse, from all walks of life, come together to work toward a common passion.

Lady Juliana ignored him for the rest of the meeting, and when it concluded she finally acknowledged his presence once more, walking over to him and placing a gloved hand on his arm.

"I must speak to Mrs. Stone about a matter. I will meet you out front shortly."

He nodded, but he saw the gleam in her eye and guessed that he was about to be challenged. He watched Lady Juliana take Mrs. Stone by the arm, drawing her away from the group and, eventually, out the door to the room beyond. Matthew caught Lady Juliana's maid, Abigail, slowly and in an obvious attempt to appear inconspicuous, leave her place and make her way to the door.

Matthew had surveyed the house upon his arrival, so he had a fairly good idea of where all of the entrances and exits were located. He left his place, ready to catch his prey.

* * *

Juliana's heart beat fast at the thought of outwitting Mr. Archibald. She knew it was foolhardy, that she should be working *with* him and not against him, but he had deliberately provoked her during the meeting. It might not have started purposely, but it had certainly ended that way.

She wasn't actually trying to escape him. She just wanted to see what might happen if she attempted to, if he would be able to find her regardless.

After thanking Mrs. Stone and telling her that she hoped no one felt uncomfortable due to her suggestion of the pamphlet, Juliana slipped out the back door and into Mrs. Stone's small garden. It was beautiful out here, and Juliana wished she could stop and spend more time appreciating the small space. Emma would most certainly love the wildflowers that were allowed to grow here, she mused. She turned the corner, ready to find James and the carriage – and ran into a wall.

"Ouch!" she cried, bouncing backward and nearly falling, except a strong arm reached out and caught her. She placed a hand on her breast and glared up at Mr. Archibald. "You startled me!"

"Oh, did I?" he said sardonically. "Perhaps if you had not been sneaking around the back that would never have occurred."

"I simply wanted to enjoy Mrs. Stone's gardens," she said with a slight toss of her head.

"Is that why you instructed your maid to wait for you in the carriage, so that you would be ready to leave without my knowledge?"

"I—" she attempted to find a witty response to that but came up empty. "I suppose I just needed a moment alone. Or, that is, a moment away from you."

"Am I really so difficult a presence?"

He said the words sarcastically, but Juliana thought she heard a hint of hurt in there, and immediately felt guilty.

"It is not *you* exactly," she said, trying to placate him, though from his expression it seemed she was only making it worse. "It is simply the feeling of entrapment. And perhaps…"

"Yes?"

"I wanted to goad you."

He stared at her incredulously for a moment and she waited for his anger, waited for him to rail at her, to tell her that she was a ridiculous child who should find something better to do with her time.

Her father would have. He had often become angry when one of them simply walked into a room, let alone said anything to him or went against his direction.

But Mr. Archibald? One corner of his lips began to move ever so slightly, curling, curling — until it turned into a smirk. Was he… laughing at her?

"You did this to *goad* me?" he asked, his lips now in a full-on grin, and Juliana couldn't help but smile sheepishly back. "You were never trying to actually run away from me?"

"No," she said, hanging her head slightly. "I've come to know you well enough to be aware that you would always be sure to find me. I merely wanted to play with you a bit after

THE SECRET OF THE DASHING DETECTIVE

you did exactly what you said you wouldn't do in that meeting."

He started laughing, shaking his head at her, and she couldn't help but chuckle back.

"Well, if nothing else," he said, "I am happy to know that you do not doubt my abilities. That would be rather disheartening."

"No, I—" Slight heat washed into her cheeks. "I actually feel quite safe with you."

"Good," he said, his smile becoming one of self-satisfaction. "I'm glad to hear it."

The air became charged between them as Juliana was suddenly flustered with embarrassment at her words, which was a relatively new concept for her. She looked up and caught Mr. Archibald's light blue eyes, which were staring at her with intensity and curiosity in equal measure.

Her breath caught and she was trapped in the moment, unsure of what to say or how to respond to him. She couldn't remember another man ever making her feel like this – so completely captivated and also somewhat unsure of herself. Was it because he was so unlike her that their differences intrigued her? Or was it something else about him as a man?

Lord Hemingway certainly didn't evoke such thoughts – of that she was certain.

She seemed to be drawn toward Mr. Archibald and when she took a short step closer to him, he didn't step away. She had no idea what was going to happen next, if he would come closer to her or—

But then a voice called out and broke down everything that had been building between them.

"My lady? Are you ready to leave?"

"James," she breathed, and looked over to the road. Mr. Archibald cleared his throat, and she turned to him, forcing a small, polite smile on her face.

"I do apologize, Mr. Archibald," she said contritely. "I should not have tried to trick you."

"No, you should not have," he agreed, but then dipped his head slightly. "And I do know I promised to stay silent in your meeting. I find it hard to do so, however, when there are potential threats to your safety."

"At least I know I can always trust you with that," she said, sweeping by him and into the carriage, afraid to remain and say any more.

CHAPTER 6

Fortunately, the duke never questioned Matthew as to where he had taken – or followed, depending on who one asked – Lady Juliana the day before. Matthew considered volunteering the information but decided that as there hadn't been much harm in the activity, it was in his best interest to maintain a cordial relationship with Lady Juliana.

This morning when Matthew arrived at Warwick House, curious as to where he would be accompanying the lady today, he found her standing just inside the front door, a bemused expression on her face.

"Mr. Archibald," she greeted him, her head swivelling back and forth as though she was watching for something – or someone. "Thank you for coming."

"Of course. Where will our travels take us today?"

She bit her bottom lip in an expression he had come to recognize as one she made when she wasn't pleased about what was to come next.

"As it happens," she said, clearing her throat slightly, "Lord Hemingway would like to escort me on a walk."

"I see," he said, unable to halt the streak of jealousy that filled his stomach. Where in all that was sacred had that come from? "And I am to follow behind like a dog?"

His comment was uncalled for – he knew it before the words even left his mouth and was all the more certain of it when her expression fell into one of dismay.

"It's not like that," she said swiftly. "Lord Hemingway came to call and requested to walk, and I thought… I thought I was only to leave the house if I was with you."

"I see," he said, taking a quick look around to make sure they were not being watched before he stepped in closer to her. "I do have one question for you, however."

"Of course," she said, her throat bobbing when she swallowed, her eyes flicking back and forth from one of his to the other as though she was nervous.

"Does he not make you feel as safe as I do?"

Her eyes widened as Matthew took a step away from her, a devilish smile on his face, and he couldn't help his grin at her speechlessness before he looked to the doorway. There was certainly no way he could keep his eyes on her any longer – not when she was staring up at him with lips parted and green eyes locked on him. He was far too likely to lean in and take those lips for himself.

Which, he was well aware, was a fantasy he needed to bury deep within himself or he was liable to lose everything he had worked so hard for.

"Mr. Archibald," she finally hissed at him, but before she could reveal whatever it was she had been about to say, footsteps sounded down the hall and a very cheerful Lord Hemingway appeared in the entrance to the foyer. He paid Matthew no attention besides a short nod, holding out his arm to Juliana and addressing only her. Not that Matthew was at all surprised. It was to be expected.

"Shall we take to the outdoors now?" Lord Hemingway asked. "You are wearing such a very lovely bonnet."

"Thank you, my lord," she responded, looking up at him with a small smile as she took his arm and stepped through the door.

She glanced back at Matthew, and he couldn't quite say what she held within her stare. He would have expected nothing less than irritation that he was following her on what was supposed to be time alone with her beau, but he wondered if there was something more there, a hint of a plea.

Perhaps she didn't enjoy Lord Hemingway's company as much as a woman should of her potential husband. Which brought him both unexpected joy and also some sadness as well. If she didn't have any desire to be in the man's presence, why on earth would she entertain a courtship with him?

Matthew followed them as they slowly meandered down Piccadilly. Any glances sent Lady Juliana's way by passersby were only those of appreciation or potential interest. He had a fair understanding of the way society worked. By promenading down one of London's best-known high-society streets, she would be practically spoken for in the scandal sheets tomorrow.

He saw Lady Juliana tilt her head and laugh at something Lord Hemingway said, the sun glinting off the soft skin on the arch of her throat. He wondered what one had to say to garner such appreciation from her, and then immediately pushed the thought from his head. What did it matter to him? He was here to see to her safety – something that he was not doing a particularly adept job at, for he was far too involved in watching her and not the environment around her.

It was the reminder he needed to take a closer look at his surroundings. It was hard to consider that a threat might exist somewhere behind the iron fenceposts of the green parks or between the red brick buildings. Here, not a hint of refuse existed in the streets – not like some of the neighbourhoods he was used to walking.

It was not as though it was a revelation. Many of his clients harkened from the Mayfair neighbourhood, not trusting the discretion of Bow Street, although Matthew himself had nothing but respect for the organization.

Which made it a mystery as to why he was suddenly so affected by the stark difference between this neighbourhood and those he belonged in. Perhaps it was Lady Juliana herself, as much as it scared him to admit the thought even to himself.

When they finally made it home after a long, boring, and uneventful walk, Matthew stood at the bottom of the steps of Warwick House as he waited for Lord Hemingway to depart. It was obvious even to Matthew that the earl was hinting to be asked in for refreshment, but Lady Juliana was either completely oblivious or attempting to appear to be so.

"It was such a lovely walk, Lord Hemingway," she said, placing a hand on his arm in what Matthew was sure was supposed to be a gesture of amiability. "Thank you ever so much."

"You are welcome, Lady Juliana," Lord Hemingway said with a wide smile. "I would be so pleased to do so again sometime soon."

"I had a lovely time," Lady Juliana said, and Matthew noted that she never specifically agreed to another outing. Warmth bloomed through his chest, and he tried to tamp it down, for he was to have no emotion toward this woman.

They said their farewells, and Matthew remained where he was, nearly as much of a fixture rooted into the ground as was the brick post next to him. Lady Juliana did not, however, forget his presence.

"Thank you, Mr. Archibald," she called out, and he had no choice but to walk up the stairs to speak to her so that it wouldn't seem too much like a princess calling down to one of those serving her – even though that was, essentially, the truth of the situation. "My apologies to waste your afternoon."

"No apologies required," he said. "You remain safe and unharmed. That is what is most important and, in fact, what I am being paid to ensure."

"I suppose that is true," she acknowledged. "But I thank you nonetheless."

He nodded and turned to go, but not before a temporary loss of sanity overtook him.

"What do you see in him?"

"P-pardon me?" she asked, her eyes wide. Matthew couldn't help but note how beautiful she looked at the moment, pink in her cheeks from the outdoors and her exertions, her bonnet just enough askew on her head of rich brown hair that it didn't look perfect, a few strands falling out to frame her face.

"Lord Hemingway. What is it that makes you wish to marry him?"

"Well, I..." she said, her hands flailing slightly in front of her as she seemed to struggle to find the words. "I am not entirely sure yet whether or not I will marry him."

"But you are obviously seriously considering it."

Why the hell was he continuing upon this discourse of conversation? It was going to give him the sack.

"I am, yes," she said faintly.

Matthew cleared his throat. "I suppose I have become invested in your safety, and I would like to ensure this man could look after you."

What a stupid sentiment, he cursed at himself. Surely she

would see through his words, words that he should never be saying to her.

"I believe that Lord Hemingway would provide me with the comforts of life that I am accustomed and also the ability to do what I have longed to for some time now."

Matthew wasn't sure that she could have hurt him worse had she stuck a blade into his chest – and he had no idea why he would possibly be so vulnerable to her words. His role was to look after Lady Juliana and assure her safety – he wasn't courting the woman.

And yet, somehow, she had worked her way into his heart, a place where she didn't belong.

"Well. I suppose if nothing else he can pay someone to look after you," Matthew said, unable to halt the hint of malice within his words. He turned to leave before his mouth betrayed him and he said something worse. He made it as far as the bottom of the stairs when she called after him.

"Mr. Archibald, are you available tomorrow?"

He turned, dismayed at the hope that sprang in his chest at the thought that she might want to see him again.

"No, actually, I am not," he said. "Your half-brother spends his Saturday afternoons at a particular pub where I am going to meet him after my morning shift here to try to come to know him better. If you need anything, I will have Mr. Green accompany you. He is the next best man for the job."

"My half-brother?" she asked, her eyes sparking with light that he had come to know meant trouble. "I am so interested in learning more about him."

"I will be sure to provide your brother all of the information I learn."

"I would most like to meet this Dr. Lewis."

Matthew fixed a look upon her. "You most certainly will not be meeting him."

She placed her hands on her hips. "Who are you, another one of my brothers?"

Matthew kept his gaze on her as he slowly climbed back up the stairs, his steps predatory as he neared. She kept her shoulders square and her stance strong as she waited for him, the air as charged between them as it always seemed to be when they were alone.

He reached out his arm, his index finger coming underneath her chin and he tilted her head up to look at him. Matthew had always been astounded by the wealth that the duke and his family possessed, uncertain of why so few people would need such expanse of land. But for once, he was glad that the house was behind a wall and a gate, for it meant that no passersby could gaze upon them with interest.

"I am many things, Lady Juliana," he said fiercely. "But one thing I most certainly am not is your brother."

And with that – and a moment he would later attribute to temporary insanity – he bent his head and took her lips with his.

He expected her to back away, to place her hands upon his chest and push him back, perhaps by slapping him across the face as she had the day he had tried to teach her to defend herself.

Which was why he was completely caught off guard when she reached up and grabbed the lapels of his jacket and pulled him in closer to her.

Her kiss was inexperienced, but her enthusiasm was not as she pressed her lips harder into him, and he couldn't help himself from tracing the seam of her lips with his tongue. She opened to him, and he slipped his tongue inside, lightly caressing hers with his. She tasted sweet, like tea and cookies, and for a moment he wondered if he could ever get enough of her.

But this one taste would have to be enough.

A voice sounded from within the house and while Juliana didn't seem to hear it, Matthew gripped her wrists as he eased back from her and slowly pushed her away.

But she didn't run. She stood and stared at him, as fixated upon him as he was on her.

"That… was…" she began, but he finished the sentence before she could.

"Something that will never happen again."

CHAPTER 7

To Juliana, the kiss had been everything. Surprising, wondrous, passionate, all that she could have ever asked for.

She knew she should have rejected it. Mr. Archibald had timed it well, the moment when they had been alone, but he was a man who worked for their family, a man who she knew she could never seriously consider. Not only that, but anyone could have seen them, standing out here on the doorstep of her family's London home. No, they couldn't be seen from the road, but they most certainly could be seen by anyone from within who happened to step outside.

None of that, however, had seemed to matter the moment his lips had descended onto hers. For despite all that her head was telling her, her soul knew that this was everything she had been waiting for, everything she hadn't realized that she needed from a man. And everything that she knew, deep in her heart, that Lord Hemingway could never be.

And then Mr. Archibald had pushed her away, not wanting anything more to do with it – with her.

A sense of rejection overwhelmed her, washing over her

in a wave – one that she whisked away as quickly as it came, allowing anger to take its place.

"You were the one who kissed me," she said now, drilling a finger into his chest, and his eyes widened in astonishment at her outburst.

"I know," he said, tilting his head downward as though he was ashamed of himself. "I shouldn't have."

"But you did. And I have a suspicion, Mr. Archibald, that you don't do anything without reason."

Emotion flashed in his eyes then, emotion that she couldn't quite name.

"Lady Juliana, I am here to do a job. I allowed myself to become caught up in the moment. It was a mistake. I should never have taken advantage of you like that."

She stepped closer to him until her nose was but an inch from his, but this time there would be no kissing. She was far too annoyed with him.

"I am not a woman who allows herself to be taken advantage of, Mr. Archibald. I do as I please," she said before adding, "within reason."

He drew a quick intake of breath, closing his eyes for a moment before fixing his light blue stare on her again.

"I do not want to complicate things, Lady Juliana," he said, his voice low, and she could hear the truth in it now. "I must think with my head. I lost my sense for a moment. I can assure you that I am now focused on what is important once more and will continue to make your protection my priority."

"My protection," she snorted, as the realization that the kiss had been such a disappointment that he had been able to 'change focus' so quickly. "That was stolen from me long ago."

"There was one difference then," he said, his mouth set in a firm line of determination. "I was not there."

The worst of it was that he was right. Keeping her safe *was* what he was getting paid to do. But it was also what his other men – Mr. Green and a man she heard called Mouse and all the rest of them – had been paid to do as well.

But she didn't feel this with any of them. This cocoon of safety, the knowledge that no matter what, as long as he was there, everything would be all right.

It was as had she said before the walk – it was never something she would feel with Lord Hemingway.

"Well," she said, swaying back and forth slightly, allowing her skirts to dance over their feet, "I should be getting in before my mother comes looking for me. I shall see you tomorrow, Mr. Archibald."

"Not tomorrow," he said, correcting her, and she nodded but didn't respond.

For she would be there tomorrow – whether he knew it or liked it or not.

* * *

"How was the princess today?"

Matthew walked into his offices to find Mouse and Anderson waiting for him.

"Don't you two have something better to do?" he grunted, rearranging the chairs back to where they belonged.

"Not particularly. We met here before going to Warwick House for our shift," Mouse said, leaning back in his seat and propping his feet up on the desk before him.

"Wonderful," Matthew said dryly. He usually enjoyed the opportunity to converse with his men, but today he didn't feel like analyzing his time with Lady Juliana. He would be doing enough of that in his own head without additional quips. "How goes the Smithfield case? Catch the wife in action yet?"

"No," Mouse said, shaking his head. "The opposite, actually. Pip just left. He said the Mrs. spent today visiting one of the foundling hospitals with a stop at her husband's mother's house on the way home. Notes are on your desk."

"Interesting," Matthew murmured as he stepped into his office, picking up the paper before him, bringing it out and reading through it. It appeared this case was not going to be how it had initially seemed. "We'll give it another week and then provide Smithfield with our report."

"Agreed," Mouse said before his lips turned up in a smirk again. "Heard you also spent some time wandering down Piccadilly following the princess and her suitor."

"I did."

"Can't say I ever thought I'd see you in such a role again."

"Part of the job. If the duke pays for me to follow his sister down Piccadilly, then down Piccadilly I walk."

"S'pose it wouldn't be so bad to watch her from behind all that way," Anderson piped in, and Matthew couldn't help the low growl that sounded in his throat.

"You will not speak of Lady Juliana that way."

When his words were met with silence, Matthew looked up from his paper to find both men staring at him with astonishment on their faces, and he found himself quickly offering an explanation.

"Her family is our client. A client that is paying us a great deal of money to watch over them and keep them safe. We will not disrespect any of them. This is the kind of business we need. Understood?"

"Understood," they both murmured, although they shared an all-knowing look before rising to make their way to Warwick House.

"Goodnight, boss."

"Goodnight."

THE SECRET OF THE DASHING DETECTIVE

* * *

"Where are you going?"

Juliana stopped with one hand on the doorknob. She paused as she tried to determine whether or not she would be able to tell her grandmother a lie, but in the end, she knew the woman would see right through her and she decided the truth was her best bet.

It was the day after Mr. Archibald had kissed her, but she was determined to push that from her mind and instead considered a matter of more importance – learning more about her half-brother.

She took a breath and turned around, grateful that her grandmother was alone. Juliana walked briskly over to where she stood in the entrance to the foyer, stopping in front of her and looking around to ensure that no one was within earshot before she began speaking, keeping her voice low and intent.

"Mr. Archibald was here watching the house this morning and I know he is now going to meet with our half-brother, Dr. Lewis, and I want to learn more about the man but Mr. Archibald doesn't want me to accompany him and Giles and Mother can never know that I'm gone."

She stopped, looking at her grandmother with supplication. Lady Winchester never even flinched.

"Don't wait long to tell Mr. Archibald you are with him, understand? Then he can at least watch over you. And stay close to him."

Juliana grinned as a rush of gratitude toward her grandmother filled her.

"Absolutely. Thank you, Grandmother."

Her grandmother nodded briskly. "I cannot say I entirely approve, but I also know that if I had a half-brother I had just learned about, I would certainly want to learn all I could about him – especially if my family was being threatened. What have you told your mother?"

"She called upon one of her friends this afternoon. I managed to avoid accompanying her by claiming a megrim, and hopefully I should be able to return before she does. I have told my maid that I am resting and do not wish to be disturbed, so if my mother does return, she will hopefully receive the message."

"You are quite surreptitious, Juliana."

"I do not mean to be," she said, feeling some chagrin and being duplicitous, but unsure what else to do.

"Very well. I won't stop you as I know if I did you would just find another way. At least it is daylight and you will be with Mr. Archibald."

Juliana couldn't help herself. She reached out and wrapped her arms around her grandmother in a quick hug, her grandmother releasing a slight "oof!" of surprise.

"I best go before I lose him," she said, and then with a wave, ran out the door.

She could still see Mr. Archibald down the street, and she quickened her footsteps as she hurried after him. She would stay within shouting distance, so as not to put herself in any danger. She could only hope that if he noticed her, they would be so far from the house that he would have no choice but to take her with him. She was aware that walking alone was to risk ruin but she would have to hope that no one noticed her. This was worth it, she thought determinedly.

She tightened the space between them as they neared the Holborn neighbourhood. She was well familiar with it, of course, having been to Mrs. Stone's house many times before.

She was just normally staring out of a carriage window, not walking at street level.

Mr. Archibald's footsteps were quick, and she had to

THE SECRET OF THE DASHING DETECTIVE

work hard to keep up, more used to leisurely strolls than a brisk walk with purpose. Finally, he stopped in front of an establishment that Juliana guessed was an inn, but in the corner was what appeared to be a pub from the noise that emanated from the door when he opened it. He slipped inside and she hurried after him, pausing in the threshold as she allowed her eyes to adjust to the dim light.

A white fireplace stood against one dark wall, while tables and benches lined the outskirts of the establishment. The place was busy enough for midafternoon hours, not as raucous as Juliana had prepared herself for, but certainly not what she was used to at a Mayfair dinner party. Her mouth dropped open as she couldn't help but stare and take in the scene, which was nothing like anything she had ever witnessed before. And yet, the more she watched, the more she noted that people still behaved like... people. There were groups of men sitting together drinking and shouting good-naturedly, and there were even a few women in the crowd, although Juliana wondered whether they were all... scrupulous.

She looked down at her own attire, grateful she had worn one of the dresses she typically donned to help Emma in the garden, a dark navy one that would hopefully prevent her from standing out, especially with her dark cloak covering it. But as she felt eyes on her, she knew that even though the garments were not new, they were of a quality that most here would have difficulty affording, and she was sure to be subject to curious glances. She'd best find Mr. Archibald before someone else found her.

She looked for his head standing tall above the crowd but had difficulty picking him out. Was he sitting down? And what about her half-brother? Would she be able to recognize him in the crowd? Would he look like her or her siblings?

She was so lost in her musings as her eyes ran around the

room that she didn't notice anyone behind her until it was too late. Hands wrapped around her upper arms, and she lashed out, trying to fight off her attacker, but the man had her in a grip too strong to break.

She was being abducted all over again.

CHAPTER 8

Matthew had been so intent on his mission here this afternoon to find this Hudson Lewis, half-brother to the Duke of Warwick and his sisters, he had completely missed the person following him so obviously that it was embarrassing.

But he had felt eyes on him when he entered the pub, and it hadn't been difficult to slip into a corner and wait for his shadow. He couldn't move his stare away from her when she entered.

Nor could any other patron.

Who wouldn't notice her? She stood out among any crowd, whether she was in Mayfair or Holborn or if she had been in the bowels of St. Giles. That was just who she was, a woman unlike any other.

And one that was causing him a fair bit of grief.

He should have been wary yesterday when he had seen that look in her eye. She was up to something. It seemed he had discovered just what that something was.

He came from behind, thinking to catch her off guard and teach her the consequences of not listening to his orders.

When he lifted his hands to her arms, he longed to wrap them around her, to hold her in his embrace and never let go, for it seemed that would be the only way to actually keep her safe.

But the moment he touched her, she stiffened immediately, and he knew that she was about to strike. He gripped her tighter, pulling her back against his chest and stilling all of the moments he had taught her as he leaned down and placed his mouth by her ear.

"You're not going to trick the man who taught you all of those moves, now are you?"

She gasped and spun around to face him as he let go of her arms. She lifted a hand and swatted him on the chest.

"Why did you do that? You have no idea how much you frightened me!"

He chuckled lowly at that, until he caught the look in her eyes. It had been more than a jest to her. She was scared – terrified, actually.

"I am sorry," he said, immediately contrite. "I never meant to scare you."

"Well, you did," she said, rubbing her arms where he had held her. "It reminded me of—never mind."

"Of when you were taken?"

"Yes."

Of course. He knew the event had affected her – it would anyone, certainly – but it seemed that it had caused her more distress than he had initially realized.

"I told you that I would keep you safe," he said intently. "And I meant it."

"I know. I believe you," she said with a trust that warmed him through before he remembered just why she was in danger today in the first place.

"There is one perfectly good way to keep you out of trouble," he couldn't help but add.

THE SECRET OF THE DASHING DETECTIVE

"Which is?"

"By you staying home in a walled mansion with guards to protect you," he said, narrowing his eyes slightly. "What were you thinking, coming here, and alone at that?"

"I'm not alone," she returned, shrugging her shoulders. "I'm with you."

He sighed, unable to help himself from reaching out and running a hand down her arm. "I have no idea what I am going to do with you," he said with a sigh, "but it seems that for today, at least, I cannot let you go anywhere without me."

She nodded, obviously pleased that her plan had worked as she had hoped. And he, the fool, was falling right into her trap. What was this woman doing to him?

He held out his arm to her, which she took with enthusiasm as he walked her through the tables, jutting his chin toward the far end of the room. "Dr. Lewis is over there. He is with a few other men so we will have to be careful about how we draw him out. It is not exactly typical for a woman to be here with a man unless she is… working, but we will have to make our excuses for you."

"Who shall we say I am?" she asked, looking up at him with green eyes that he could lose himself in. He shook his head to loosen himself from the stupor she had placed over him. "Your sister?"

"No," he said immediately. That would never work. Not if anyone noticed how he looked at her. He couldn't help himself. As much as he tried to deny it, he was finally able to admit that he wanted her with every ounce of his being. Not that he would act upon it again – that had been undeniably foolish – though that made the longing all the worse.

"You will have to be my wife."

He didn't like how her eyes gleamed at that, nor how it caused a fair bit of excitement within his own heart.

"That sounds fun. I've never been a wife before."

"Just to meet with Dr. Lewis," he said, hoping she heard the warning in his tone.

"Of course."

They took a seat at a table near him, and he saw how Juliana's eyes kept flicking over to the men as she tried without any success not to stare.

"Which one is he?" she hissed, and Matthew nearly rolled his eyes. This woman would make no spy, that was for certain.

"With the brown cap," Matthew murmured as he took a sip of the ale the barmaid had brought over for them. Juliana eyed the cup in front of her with a mixture of interest and uncertainty, and Matthew couldn't help the smile that played on his lips as she leaned in and delicately sniffed it.

"What is this?" she asked, pushing a stray tendril of chestnut hair behind her ear.

"Ale."

"Right."

"Have you ever drunk ale before?"

"No."

"Go slowly," was all he had to offer as he sat back and waited for the entertainment.

She didn't disappoint as she wrapped both of her hands around the large cup and lifted it to her mouth.

She took one quick sip before her eyes widened and she had to cover her mouth as she obviously forced herself to swallow it down. He saw her eyes water as she tried not to grimace.

"How is it?" he asked, hiding his grin behind his own mug.

"It is... different."

"I can imagine," he said, admiring her bravery as she reached down and tried once more. This time it seemed to go a slight bit easier, although he imagined it was a far cry from the sugary sweet drinks of her London events or the fine wine that was served at the duke's dinner table.

There were three men with Lewis, and Matthew wondered just how they were going to get to the man.

He knew a bit about him from facts provided by Owen, who had been watching him for some time now. The man was single and lived on his own nearby.

"Do you have anything wrong with you?" Matthew asked Juliana in a low voice. Her eyes widened as she sat back in her seat, placing the ale down on the table before her.

"What do you mean by that? I suppose one could say there are loads of things wrong with me. As to just *what* is wrong would depend on who you ask."

"I mean, do you have any ailments? Anything a physician might be able to help with?"

"No, I do not think so."

"We'll have to make something up, then."

When one of the men from the table next to them rose to join a different group, Matthew saw his chance and leaned in toward Lewis.

"Doc? That is, are you a doctor?"

Lewis turned and looked at him, and Matthew could immediately see the man's resemblance to the duke. The ladies, Juliana and Prudence, looked more like their mother with their chestnut hair and green eyes, but the duke – and this man – must take after their father. Matthew had a feeling that the resemblance likely haunted the duke.

"Yes," Lewis said, his demeanour instantly changing from a man having a drink with friends to a professional. "Is something wrong?"

"My wife here is having some stomach upset, and I was wondering if you had any thought to the cause or perhaps some recommendations. Would you have a moment to sit with us? I'll pay you for your time."

Lewis turned back to his friends and made his excuses before taking a seat next to Lady Juliana, across the table from Matthew. Lady Juliana's eyes widened as she looked both fascinated and nervous at the thought she was sitting next to a brother she had never known.

"I'll do what I can to help, but it's probably best if you visit my office or have me call upon you," Lewis said. "I would be much better prepared."

"I understand, and I'm sorry, Doc. Truly I am," Matthew said with a sheepish grin, while he noticed that Lady Juliana still couldn't stop staring at the man with undisguised curiosity. He nudged her with his foot underneath the table, hoping she would understand to stop. "It's just, my wife is in a bit of pain and has had a few issues lately. I'm just not sure what to do."

"Very well" Lewis said, looking at Lady Juliana now, and she stared back. "What seems to be the problem? Do you have any other symptoms?"

"Ah…" she began, looking to Matthew for help, and he nodded at her encouragingly. She was the one who wanted to be here. Now she would have to help him as best she could. "Y-yes, I have stomach upset. It comes and goes. And I am very tired. All the time."

"I see," Lewis said, revealing no emotion. "Anything else?"

"Ummm…" she said, tapping her fingers on the table in a show of nerves," that is mostly all."

"When were your last courses?"

"Pardon me?" Lady Juliana asked, her cheeks turning pink.

Lewis patted her shoulder as a grandfather would his grandchild in sympathy.

"I only ask because I am trying to determine if the obvious answer is the correct one. The symptoms you are

THE SECRET OF THE DASHING DETECTIVE

describing are often those a woman would feel if she was with child."

If it was possible, Lady Juliana's cheeks turned an even brighter red, and it took everything within Matthew not to burst into laughter as she looked to him in desperation. "I ah, I see," she managed. "Yes, I-I suppose that could be the case."

"Well, congratulations to you both," Lewis said, reaching across the table and shaking Matthew's hand. Matthew allowed the grin to cross his face, for he should be as pleased as any expectant father, should he not? Truth be told, the notion of having a child with Juliana… well it was not as absurd as he would have thought. In fact, it was rather… interesting.

"Thank you," Matthew said, reaching into his pocket for a shilling. "Is this enough for your time?"

Lewis held up a hand, rejecting it. "No need. It was nothing."

"I insist."

"Absolutely not."

"Allow me to buy you a drink, then."

"Very well," Lewis said, before turning to Lady Juliana again. "You are both welcome to come see me again if needed, although I would propose that you are better off with a midwife who knows much more about such matters than I do. If you need any suggestions, please tell me and I will be happy to provide you with a few names."

"That would be lovely," Lady Juliana said, the pink in her cheeks having receded, to be replaced with some warmth in her face as she stared at the man who was, apparently, her brother. "You are quite kind."

Lewis grinned. "I endeavor to be so."

He looked to Matthew now.

"How did you know I was a physician? I do not believe I've ever met you before."

Matthew shrugged. "Word gets around. You know how it is."

"I do. I believe I've seen you in here, although I've never made your acquaintance."

Matthew nodded. He thought of giving the man a fake name, but then decided it was better not to. Having lived his entire life in Holborn, it wouldn't be long until Lewis discovered his true identity.

"Matthew Archibald," he introduced himself. "You're not from around here, are you, Dr. Lewis?"

"I'm not, actually," Lewis said. "I grew up in a town not far from London until I came here for my schooling. I've remained ever since."

"Do you like it here?" Lady Juliana asked, chiming in, still obviously fascinated by the man. "As opposed to where you are from?"

"I suppose it's certainly a different world," Lewis said, his eyes somewhat faraway. "In a small town, everyone knows you. Here you are more anonymous, which can be both comforting and isolating."

Matthew wondered how much being born a bastard had affected Lewis' childhood, especially in a town where one couldn't hide the fact he had no father.

"Well, I am glad you are here," Lady Juliana said, leaning in toward him. "You are an asset to London."

Apparently, Lady Juliana had made her decision as to whether or not to trust her half-brother. While Lewis seemed a good sort, Matthew was still wary. It was also why he had wanted to meet Lewis himself first – he had a feeling that none of the siblings would be able to be particularly impartial. Especially Lady Juliana.

"I was about to eat," Lewis said. "Would you like to join me?"

"Why not?" Matthew said, eager to take whatever opportunity he could to get to know the man better. His mother wouldn't be pleased when he showed up to family dinner with a full stomach, but sometimes a man had to do what he had to do.

He saw Lady Juliana begin to shake her head desperately, and he wondered what was bothering her, but he couldn't help her. She was the one who had wanted to join him.

Matthew signaled to the barmaid, telling her that they wanted the luncheon special. She nodded and soon returned with three plates.

Which was when Matthew realized why Lady Juliana hadn't wanted to stay. She looked down at the food, her face now green. Interesting, how practically a rainbow of colors had crossed it today.

He followed her gaze to her plate, where a leg of mutton sat staring up at her. She looked at Matthew and he wondered if she was about to be sick.

"I cannot eat this," she said in a loud whisper to him. Matthew opened his mouth to encourage her, but Lewis spoke first.

"Another sign you are with child," he said kindly. "Food that is typically appetizing suddenly loses all of its appeal."

Juliana nodded before looking over at Matthew, her face still twisted in sickness. "Please take it away."

He nodded, moving it to his side of the table. He picked up his spoon and transferred all of the peas in sauce from his plate to hers while he took her meat. "How do the peas appeal to you, darling?" he asked, and she nodded gratefully.

"Much better."

"There you are, then," he said, passing her the plate, feeling nearly like a true husband at his ability to take care of her, even in something so minute.

Which was quite frightening indeed.

CHAPTER 9

They passed the rest of the meal conversing in relative ease, and Matthew was surprised at how much he actually liked Lewis. By the end of it, he was feeling rather disquieted for deceiving him, although he reminded himself that he was doing a job, not making a friend – even though it would be simple to do so with Lewis.

He also noted that while Lewis spoke easily and without any malice, he also didn't provide them much information as to his background, although he did tell them that he went to school at St. Bart's, which wouldn't have been possible without a fair bit of financial backing – which took him back to the very reason they knew of Lewis' existence. The duke had found payments in his father's ledgers to a Mrs. Lewis that had been made regularly for years – payments which she had obviously saved for her son's education. He wondered how much Lewis knew about them.

"Well, we best be going," Matthew finally said, standing and holding his arm out to Lady Juliana. He insisted on paying for the meal, telling Lewis that he hoped to see him again. Lewis smiled and nodded, wished them luck once again, and bid them farewell.

As Matthew walked out of the pub with Lady Juliana on his arm, he became rather worried. For all of this – a meal with a wife and a friend – seemed much preferable to the truth.

Lady Juliana clutched Matthew's arm as they left the pub and started down the road back toward Mayfair. She was so awash in emotion that it seemed to take her a moment to realize where they were.

"Do you live close to here?"

"I do."

"Were you planning on returning to Warwick House?"

"No."

"So I am taking you far out of your way," she stated, and he shrugged.

"Think nothing of it."

Of course, that didn't seem to help as she pursed her lips.

"Dr. Lewis was a lovely man, wasn't he?"

Matthew looked down at her, at the way her eyes were glowing, and she returned his stare.

"What's wrong?" she asked, obviously catching the conflict in his eyes, and Matthew tightened his lips together as his gaze left her and fixated on the road in front of them.

"What is wrong is that you are right. He did seem like a good man. If that is the case, it means I am no closer to determining who is threatening your family."

"I must tell you, Mr. Archibald, I do pride myself on being a fairly good judge of character, and I just do not think that Dr. Lewis could have been the one who abducted me or who tried to kill Giles. He is a physician. He heals people. And he was so kind and amiable. It is just not possible."

Matthew stopped, drawing Lady Juliana over to the side

of the road, his hands on her forearms to keep her close to him and out of harm's way.

"I know you are viewing him as family, and he does seem a good man. But we have to remain impartial. I have seen many men who appear to be good do unthinkable acts for reasons we cannot comprehend. I just… I do not want to see you disappointed, my lady."

She nodded, even as he could see the dismay on her face. He hated to cause her any distress, but he also knew that it was better she be prepared. She stepped in closer to him, tilting her face up toward him.

"Can I ask you something?"

"I have a feeling you are going to no matter how I answer that."

"Please do not call me my lady, or even Lady Juliana. When it is just the two of us… Juliana will do."

She looked down suddenly, but not before he caught the slight blush steal across her cheeks.

"I am not sure that is wise."

"Perhaps not," she said, her gaze fixated somewhere in the middle of his chest now. "But I feel that we have been through a great deal together, and it seems… right."

He wanted to tell her no, to push her as far away from him as possible, before either of them caught hold of any emotion that would lead nowhere. But it didn't seem to be within him to deny her at the moment.

"Very well," he said with a quick nod. "Matthew will do – when we are alone. And only then."

She nodded. "Thank you, Matthew."

Then his heart responded to her smile, and it was at that moment he knew he was in trouble.

* * *

THE SECRET OF THE DASHING DETECTIVE

JULIANA WAS aware that Matthew likely didn't even realize that his hands had tightened on her arms. She wished he was holding her for an altogether different reason, but she would enjoy the moment for what it was.

It had, so far, been the most wonderful afternoon. She had met the brother she had never even known existed until a short time ago, and he seemed kind and gentleman-like, and she wanted to believe in him. He had done nothing wrong but been sired by the same father as she. He likely didn't even know there was noble blood in his veins.

As for Matthew... she would make sure that he didn't regret the closeness that had grown between them. She knew this connection was impossible, yet she couldn't help her need to explore it, to understand why it was so strong with him and no one else.

He looked around them suddenly as though just realizing where they were and that he did have to take her home and began to hurry her away. Before they got far, however, she heard a voice call out his name, and Juliana turned to the sound even while he tried to continue on as though he hadn't heard anything at all.

"Matthew?" she said, tugging on his arm as he continued to walk. "Matthew, I believe that woman is calling for you."

A woman stood outside the doorway of one of the small townhouses, a baby clutched in one of her arms while the other one waved wildly at them.

"Matthew, wait a moment! We shall be out shortly. Tom, come, Matthew is here!"

Juliana turned toward Matthew, who seemed resigned now as he stood and stared at the door of the building, hands in his pockets.

"Do you know them?"

"Yes," he said. "That is my sister."

"Oh, how wonderful," Juliana said with glee, eager to meet

a member of Matthew's family. It felt like he knew absolutely everything about her while she knew hardly a thing about him. She waited with anticipation while the woman and her family neared.

"Matthew, I am so glad you came by for us," the woman said. She resembled Matthew, her hair the same sandy shade, pulled back from her face as she juggled the infant, who appeared to be about six months old, in her arms. She grinned widely at Juliana.

"I am Betsy. Matthew's sister."

"It is lovely to meet you," Juliana said enthusiastically. "I am L—Juliana."

"I am equally pleased to meet you, Juliana," Betsy said. "This is my husband, Tom, and our baby, Andrew."

"He is so very sweet," Juliana said, but before she could continue, Matthew stepped between them.

"I was just returning Juliana home, and then I will meet you," he said to Betsy. "Tell Mother apologies for my lateness."

Juliana looked at him in dismay. "I am keeping you from an engagement?"

"Just dinner with my family."

"You should join us," Betsy suggested, and Juliana responded with, "I'd love to!" just as Matthew ground out, "Absolutely not."

"I do not mean to intrude, but if I am welcome, I would be most interested in accompanying you." She stopped as her face heated again, and she regretted her pale cheeks and their propensity to show her every emotion. "That is, if I would be invited."

"Of course. Guests are always welcome at my mother's dinner table," Betsy said, but Matthew, of course, was already shaking his head.

"You wouldn't be interested," he said, "and your family will wonder where you are."

Juliana placed her hands on her hips.

"On the contrary. I would be most pleased to meet your family and share a meal. I shall send a note to my brother telling him I have a dinner engagement, if he is even interested as he will likely be preoccupied with Emma. She is expecting and Giles is quite attentive. Besides, Emma will come up with an excuse for me if it is required, as long as she knows that I am safe — which I am, for I am with you. My mother and sister are out for the evening, so they will not even notice." She decided that Matthew was no longer welcome to have an opinion in this and turned to Betsy. "How far do we have to go?"

Betsy appeared to be quite enjoying their exchange.

"It is not far at all. Just around the corner. Mother will be *most* excited to meet you."

Juliana stole a glance at Matthew, who appeared rather pained, but he seemed to have accepted the fact that there wasn't much he could do about the situation now that Betsy and Juliana had started forward. Juliana saw Tom clap a hand on his shoulder in solidarity, and she had to laugh even as she wondered if this was the best of ideas.

But she was too interested in what was awaiting her to question it any further.

Betsy chatted amiably with her about everything and nothing as they made their way down the wide street and turned the corner to a much narrower road with doorways rather close together. Matthew said nothing at all until they arrived at a small home on the corner, which looked remarkably well kept and quite comfortable. They didn't knock on the door but instead Matthew walked right in. With only the slightest of hesitations, Juliana stepped in front of him when he held the door open for her, only to be greeted by a cacophony of smells and voices.

"There you are!"

A tall, statuesque woman wielding a wooden spoon came toward the front entrance to greet them. She hugged Betsy, kissed the baby, patted Tom, and swatted Matthew all in seemingly one motion before her eyes came to rest on Juliana.

"And just who do we have here?"

"Juliana," she said, introducing herself when it seemed that Matthew had lost his voice. "I hope you do not mind that I have invited myself to your home."

"Nonsense," Betsy said, waving a hand before walking deeper into the sitting area of the house. "I invited you."

"You are welcome, my dear," the woman said, although she was obviously quite interested in just what Juliana's connection was to any of her children. "I haven't seen you around before and I've lived here all of my life. When did you meet Betsy?"

"About five minutes ago," Juliana said with a smile. "Matthew was escorting me home and Betsy and Tom happened upon us."

"Well, I am certainly glad they did," she said with a warm smile, although she obviously had a number of questions for her son, who stood like a brooding statue behind her.

Juliana turned toward him. "Would it be possible to send the note round? I shall tell my brother I have remained with Lady Maria to dine tonight."

"You have certainly been spending a lot of time with Lady Maria," he said with the first sign of humour on his face since they had run into Betsy, and Juliana couldn't help but chuckle herself.

"I suppose I shall have to call upon her and tell her that I have been using her as an excuse. I have no idea if she will help me or not as that seems fairly terrible of me, but I best try."

A man who must be Matthew's father came in and greeted them, taking her cloak.

"Mr. Archibald," Juliana greeted him, and he waved her words away.

"Call me Henry. And welcome to our home."

Matthew led her into the small sitting area, which was full of people who must be his siblings and their spouses, while children were playing with various dolls and other wooden toys on the floor before them. It was noisy, boisterous, and so different from any meal Juliana had ever attended before.

She loved it.

"I know this is a far cry from Mayfair," Matthew murmured in her ear, but she shook her head as a smile bloomed across her face.

"This is wonderful," she said, meaning it with all of her heart. She could already tell there was such love in this room, and she had only just walked in.

When Matthew left to write and send her note, Betsy waved her in and patted the seat next to her on the worn, yet comfortable, sofa. The furniture was situated around a brown brick fireplace, in which a large fire burned merrily in the hearth.

Betsy introduced their other sister Mary, and her husband, Phillip, as well as another brother, George, and his wife, Sarah.

She also told Juliana the names of about six children on the floor who ranged in age from a small toddler to a child of about seven, but by then Juliana had lost the capacity to remember which name belonged to which child.

Despite the animated conversation around them, Juliana could feel Matthew's presence when he re-entered the room, and her head turned, seeking him out even though she didn't mean to do so.

His eyes caught hers, and the intensity in them was nearly more than she could bear.

It seemed that his family noticed too, as Juliana realized the conversation began to slow around them.

Finally, his mother eased the tension by announcing dinner.

Juliana waited to see who would go in to eat first – for surely all of these people couldn't fit in the kitchen at the same time? But they seemed to have their own sense of order as they fed the children first and then arranged them in a circle on the floor.

They all crowded around the wooden table that had obviously been present for many years to witness the family grow. It took up nearly the entirety of the dining room and the chairs were squished as close together as possible, but no one seemed to have any concern.

They insisted that Juliana, as their guest, be served first of the adults, and when she reached for the dish, she was immediately as nervous as she had been her first time at a society dinner.

Fortunately, Matthew was right there next to her, passing her a plate and providing her with some helpful suggestions as to which dishes contained meat and which she would feel comfortable eating. Which, once his family heard, sparked some lively conversation.

"You do not eat meat?" Mary asked, her eyes wide, and Juliana shook her head.

"What about poultry?"

"What about fish?"

"What about eggs?"

The questions continued to be fired toward her, and Juliana couldn't help but laugh at their curiosity until

Matthew finally threw his hands up in the air and told them all that was quite enough. They settled down once everyone's plates were full from the seemingly never-ending supply of food.

It also seemed that none of Matthew's family cared about which utensils Juliana used to eat or what she drank – as long as the glass was full in front of her – nor whether she ate quickly or slowly or somewhere in between.

They accepted her as she was.

And Juliana wasn't sure if she had ever been more grateful.

CHAPTER 10

Matthew couldn't move his eyes away from Juliana as she sat with his family. He had been concerned about how she would fit in, what she would think of them all, and whether she would look down at them and their lifestyle, so different from her own.

But instead, she seemed to belong here.

He had no idea what to think of it.

She sat across the table from him, wedged between his sisters, who seemed to have taken her in as one of their own.

She was breathtaking. In the dim candlelight, her cheeks were flushed, from either the warmth of the room or the conversation around her, he wasn't certain. Tendrils of her chestnut hair brushed against the side of her face and her red lips had curled into a wide smile as she laughed at something his brother said. Matthew had been too caught up in watching her to even listen.

"She's wonderful."

Matthew turned to his mother, who was sitting next to him with a knowing smile on her face.

"She's not for me," he said gruffly, not meeting her eye.

"Why would you say that?" his mother asked, studying him.

"Trust me," he said. "We are from different worlds. I do not belong in hers, nor she in mine."

"It seems to me that she is fitting in just fine. A bit odd with the meat thing, but I can see past that."

Matthew snorted.

"She is comfortable for an evening, but it could never be much beyond that." He tried to hide his sigh by lifting his glass and then taking a sip of the drink. "I never would have brought her here, truly I wouldn't have, but Betsy saw me escorting her home and insisted. Juliana couldn't help but want to come."

"Her eyes stay on you."

He shook his head. He couldn't allow his mother to raise her hopes.

"You know I only want for you to be happy," his mother said, patting his hand, and he couldn't help his smile for her.

"I know you do," he said, allowing some of his reservations to fall as his tone softened. "And you know how much I love you for it."

"I do."

"Please don't place your hopes in Juliana," he said. "She's not the woman for me."

"I am beginning to believe otherwise, but I will keep my opinions to myself as you clearly have not asked for them," she said. "For now, know she is welcome here with our family anytime you choose to bring her."

"Thank you, Mother," he said quietly.

The rest of the evening passed rather quickly. Eventually Matthew was able to shake the sullenness that had overcome him. He supposed his melancholy stemmed from the fact that his mother was right. Juliana *did* seem to belong here, and there was a part of him that could picture her making her home with him, leaving all behind for the life that he could provide her.

But she was the sister of a duke, he reminded himself. She would never be for him, and he best get used to it.

He had no other choice.

* * *

Juliana was floating on air as they walked home.

"Your family is so wonderful, Matthew," she said, squeezing his arm. He had been reluctant to walk her home alone in the dark, but he didn't have much choice.

"They can be overwhelming sometimes."

"Not at all!" she exclaimed. "You have come to know my family. They are lovely but there is not that same feeling of… kinship that your family has."

"We are from different worlds, which is obvious."

"What does that matter?" she asked, turning to him. "That does not mean we cannot enjoy spending time with people who are new to us. And I *did* enjoy spending time with your family. I would like to do so again."

"I do not think that's a good idea.

"Why not?"

His jaw hardened once more into that granite stare, and she sighed, knowing she wasn't going to get far with him.

"What reason could there possibly be for you getting close to them?" He asked.

"Because I like them," she said, wondering why he was being so surly. She decided that she'd had quite enough of it. She stopped walking and stood in front of him, her hands on her hips.

"What is wrong with you?" she asked, poking him in the chest. "We just had a lovely dinner, and you are here being nothing but difficult."

He stared over her shoulder as if he didn't want to meet her gaze.

"You must trust me that this is for your own good."

"Do I not have the ability to decide that for myself?"

His blue eyes finally lowered to hers, and she forgot where she was, what they were doing, that there were people moving past them.

"You want to know why?"

"That is what I am asking you."

"Fine," he said, and the control that he always held so carefully seemed to snap. "I do not want you to come too close because you and I cannot *be* anything together. We are from different worlds. You are to marry Lord what's-his-name and would have no interest in leaving your privileged life to join mine. I do not see what benefit there would be in the two of us spending time together, of you becoming familiar with my *family*, only for us to part ways eventually. One of us will be hurt. Both of us might be hurt. Whatever happens, it is best to stop it now, before it even starts."

When he finished, his breaths were coming deeply, and he took a step back as though he had surprised himself with his reaction. Juliana couldn't help but reach out a hand and slide it up the side of his face.

"I didn't realize you felt like that."

"I should have no feeling toward you."

"But you *do*," she said, the thought filling her with warmth that blossomed out from her chest. "I thought... I thought you were repelled by me."

"Why would you ever think that?" he asked incredulously.

"You told me that the kiss could never happen again. I thought I had been so terrible that you never wanted to repeat it because I was too inexperienced and that you were... repelled by me."

He stepped toward her, wrapping his hands around her shoulders.

"*Never* think that," he said fiercely. "You are... amazing. Don't ever let yourself feel otherwise."

Hope sparked in Juliana's chest, and she looked up at him in impish glee. "So it wasn't a horrible kiss?"

"No."

"Would you care to repeat it?"

His eyes flicked back and forth from one of hers to the other.

"We cannot."

"Why?"

"I told you why."

"And I am telling you that whatever happens, we will figure it out when the time comes."

"That is easy for you to say."

"Why?" she challenged him. "Do you not understand that I feel as you do? That all this time I wondered what was missing with Lord Hemingway and then I found that missing piece is there whenever I'm with you? He is a nice enough man, but there are plenty of nice men out there. Neither he nor anyone else has ever made me *feel* as you do. Like we fit together, that there is a spark between us that is impossible to deny. Let's explore it and see where it takes us."

His eyes shuttered closed for a moment and when he opened them and stared at her, his face nearing hers, she knew that she had captured him.

"This is a terrible idea," he muttered.

"Perhaps."

"We really should stop this before it even begins."

"So you say."

"But..."

And then his lips were on hers once more and Juliana sank

into it, opening her mouth to him, remembering all from last time, as she was once again overwhelmed by the sensations that flooded over her. The taste of him, like after-dinner cake mixed with a uniquely masculine appeal; the scent of him, like wood shavings and musk; the feel of his strong chest muscles beneath her hands and under his shirt and jacket.

She was so wrapped up in him that she forgot where they were until the whistle of a passerby interrupted them and they finally separated. Only it was no jumping away in regret. It was a separation with a smile on their faces at what they had just shared together.

And this time, she had a feeling that it was going to be happening again.

* * *

Matthew had always enjoyed his job.

But the next two weeks with Juliana were some of the most pleasurable he could ever remember.

He accompanied her wherever she wished to go. Some of the events were, of course, rather boring, but most of what she did was quite admirable. There were meetings at Mrs. Stone's house, as well as work on her pamphlet. Juliana and Matthew actually spent a fair amount of time in one of the small parlors of Warwick House, Juliana amalgamating all of the information the other members of her society provided her while she instructed Matthew on the drawings she would need to accompany the words.

It had been some time since he had done any sketching or illustrating, and he quite enjoyed doing so again – especially when Juliana seemed so enthusiastic about his work. Even Prudence had spent some time with them, curious about what was keeping them occupied. Matthew had an inkling that her approval was hard to come by, so he was appreciative when she praised his skill.

He couldn't remember ever completing a task like this before, and he wasn't sure if he enjoyed the work, or if it was the time with Juliana – or both.

He didn't forget the threat to her family. How could he, when all he wanted to do during his every waking moment was keep her safe? But with most of his attention focused on Juliana, Matthew found that he had to – for now – trust his men to continue doing the work of following up on the case itself. Owen was looking into a few leads, but so far they had determined that both Hemingway and Lewis were fairly innocuous. They were still keeping an eye on them, but in the meantime had turned to the previous duke and any enemies he might have had.

Which proved to be a mountainous task.

The current Duke of Warwick had nearly been unable to stop laughing when Matthew had asked if his father had any enemies. The duke told him the better question was who had his father *not* insulted in some form during his lifetime.

Which amounted in a fair number of additional suspects. Matthew had his men running through them, not missing their barbs about how he was living the good life while they did all of the hard work.

Which was partially true.

"Would you come with me tomorrow to Cheapside?" Juliana asked, looking up at him from her writing desk across the room.

"Cheapside?" he said with a frown. "What is in Cheapside?"

"We are going to be walking through the area, feeding stray dogs as well as seeing to their welfare. If any of them need any help that cannot be provided in the street, we will try to take them with us to give them the care they need to survive."

"I see," Matthew said, even though he didn't at all. "Just what will you do with those who do need help?"

"The vicar and his wife have agreed to start a small sanctuary of sorts for animals in the yard beyond their church. It won't be much, but it will be a start. The vicar has built a small building for the dogs already! And if there are too many, well, I suppose a few of us can take additional dogs home."

The corner of Matthew's lips twitched as he wondered just what the duke would have to say about that.

"What does your brother think?"

"I would never tell him this is what I have planned," Juliana said in horror.

"Do you not think he will notice if you showed up with a stray dog in tow?"

"Matthew," Juliana said without blinking. "Sometimes, when you know that someone is not going to give you the answer that you need or want to hear, it is better to go ahead and do what you need to do and then request forgiveness later."

"I see," he said, thinking back to her appearance at the pub to meet with Lewis. "I shall have to remember that."

She nodded briskly and then returned to the paper before her.

Matthew could only shake his head as he returned to his own work – while wondering if he would ever tire of this woman.

CHAPTER 11

"Are you sure this is a good idea?" Prudence asked, eyeing Juliana and her attire as she stood in the foyer and waited for Matthew to arrive. "I know that you want to help and all, and I do appreciate that about you, but this seems somewhat... extreme."

"It is just fine, Pru," Juliana said, placing a hand on her shoulder. "Abigail is accompanying us as well, so we will have plenty of hands. But yours are always welcome."

Prudence shook her head, looking pained by the thought as she looked sympathetically at Abigail, who waited against the wall. "I would be more likely to have my hand bitten off by one of the creatures."

Juliana rolled her eyes. Prudence enjoyed animals in her own way, but she was also much more timid when it came to trusting them.

"I shall bring you home a stray of your own."

"Please don't. Giles will have an apoplexy, to say nothing of what Mother would think."

"What would Mother think?" Their mother appeared in the doorway and Juliana nearly groaned aloud. If only

Matthew had been on time, they could have been out of here before her mother had noticed anything.

"Mother would think that it is a fine day to take to the outdoors," Juliana said, forcing a smile. "I had better go!"

"What in heaven's name are you wearing?" her mother said, her eyes wide as she must have caught sight of the attire Juliana tried to hide beneath her cloak.

"I am going to take a turn about the gardens, and thought I best not wear anything that might get snagged on an errant branch," Juliana said, which was true. She *was* first going to go feed her animals. She had her bag of kitchen scraps tucked beneath her cloak. Today, however, she was going to walk around the outside of the fence to see if she could entice any of them to come closer to her. She was well aware just how filthy her garments would likely become.

"I shall see you soon. Good afternoon!"

As she caught sight of Matthew's profile, she slipped through the door, nearly forgetting Abigail in the process, but the girl, ever vigilant since Juliana had been abducted while she had been watching, quickly followed her out the door and down the steps. Juliana wished she could jump over the last step and into Matthew's arms, greeting him with the kiss she had dreamed about last night, but it would have to remain a dream for now. Taking her fill of him with her eyes would have to suffice.

Sometimes she nearly couldn't believe that she found a connection with such a man. She knew he was right when he said that there could never be anything more between them besides stolen kisses and gazes of longing, but the impulsiveness within her just couldn't turn away from him. When they were apart, she wanted nothing more than for them to be together again. She looked forward to their meeting each day with indescribable anticipation, and as much as she had no wish for her family to be in danger, she couldn't help that small part of herself that was grateful there was a reason for them to continue to see one another.

She just had to be certain that her family never discovered any of this or she knew her mother would very quickly put a quick stop to it.

Juliana looked Matthew up and down, delighting in the fact that he had obviously not worn his best clothing for the day.

"You are going to help with our efforts!"

He eyed her with some reluctance.

"I couldn't shake this feeling that you might need rescuing today, so I dressed accordingly."

She couldn't help but laugh at that as the carriage rolled around to the front of the house. She allowed Matthew to help first her and then Abigail into the carriage, and then she reached out the door and placed a hand on Matthew's chest before he joined James up top.

"Will you ask James to circle behind Warwick House first, please?"

"Behind?" he frowned. "Why?"

"I haven't yet fed the dogs today, and I was hoping to get closer to them first – to see if they will come to me without bars between us and if there is anything else that I can do for them before we continue on to Cheapside. How can I offer help to strange dogs when I haven't done more for those I consider like my own?"

"Very well," Matthew said before climbing atop. Juliana had previously suggested he ride in the carriage with her, but he always refused, telling her that he had a better view of any impending threats when he sat up with James, the coachman. She also suspected he was reluctant to go where he felt he didn't belong, which she didn't quite understand. If she – and Abigail – were the only ones in the carriage, then what did it matter what anyone else thought?

She didn't push him any further on it, however, figuring that he had his own reasons for making such decisions.

The carriage turned around the corner and Juliana smiled when she looked out the window and saw that her dogs were already lined up along the fence, waiting for her. James pulled the carriage to a stop a few paces away, and Matthew helped Juliana out of the carriage. She passed him a few pieces of tough chicken, which he took without comment and she considered his silence his acceptance in following along with her.

They approached the dogs slowly, and Juliana reached out an arm to halt Matthew's progress before they came too close.

"We don't want to scare them," she whispered.

He nodded his assent and Juliana lightly clicked her tongue against the roof of her mouth. Lucy turned first, her right ear lifting as it usually did while her left remained where it was. She tilted her head in confused recognition when she saw Juliana was standing on the same side of the fence as she was. Juliana knelt and held her hand out, hoping that Lucy would understand that she wasn't a threat.

"Here, girl," she said softly. "Would you like some?"

Lucy took one hesitant step forward and then another, but before she could make it all the way to Juliana, another dog – a big shaggy brute who Juliana had named Max – came bounding along beside her to Matthew. Matthew, unfortunately, was not holding the food out before him, but instead still had it clenched in his hand held near his chest. Max took one look at him and then pounced on Matthew, knocking him down and placing his paws on Matthew's shoulders before he began nuzzling his hands in search of the food.

Once Juliana became aware that Matthew wasn't hurt, she couldn't help but let out a giggle at his plight – but when she turned around to look for Lucy and found her gone, her smile instantly fled.

The dog had been scared off – and seemed to be nowhere else in sight.

"We'll return later."

Matthew had somehow found his footing and risen onto his haunches, for he was now kneeling next to her, his warm, low voice in her ear.

"She likely won't be here," Juliana said, unable to help the melancholy in her tone. "She only comes here mid-morning, and now we might have scared her off forever."

"I doubt that," Matthew said, placing a comforting hand on her shoulder. "She knows that you'll be here for her, and we didn't do anything that harmed her in any way. She'll be back."

He patted her shoulder one more time as though he wasn't entirely sure what to do with his hand, before he rose to his feet.

"Come now," he said, holding out a hand, "we have the dogs of Cheapside to save."

* * *

They were such an odd gathering, standing around in a grouping together. All were of varying ages, economics, and completely different walks of life.

Yet, in some ways, Matthew was aware that they had more in common than many groups of people who gathered together for more social of situations.

They were armed with plenty of scraps of food as well as a few ropes to capture the dogs if necessary. None of them actually held a weapon of any sort, as far as Matthew could tell.

"Did anyone bring a knife? Or a pistol?"

They all stared at him as though he had suggested that they should use the weapons to shoot him on the spot.

"Matthew," Juliana exclaimed, stepping forward and speaking for them all, "why would we ever bring weapons? We are here to *help* the animals, not to hurt them!"

"I was actually more considering how you might protect yourselves from anyone who might try to stop you – although it is also likely a good idea to have some protection against a dog who considers you a threat – or lunch."

"Matthew!" Juliana protested, and he nearly had to roll his eyes at her naivety.

He supposed that was why he was here.

"Not to worry," he said, double checking that he had his knife in his belt, his pistol at his back, and a dagger in his boot.

Matthew sighed in resignation as the group before him began to spread out, looking down side alleys and in the corners between buildings – everywhere that he would have told them to avoid.

He should have brought more of his men.

But, he told himself, besides Juliana, none of the rest of them were any of his concern. Except that he couldn't help that he had started to feel a great deal of admiration for each of the people he had watched in meetings over the past few weeks. He would keep his eyes on Juliana, but that didn't mean he wouldn't do all he could to ensure the safety of the entirety of the group.

Juliana had paired with Miss Polley, who followed Juliana much more timidly down the street. Juliana took her arm exuberantly and led her down to a small square.

"We should find a butcher shop."

"Why a butcher shop?" Miss Polley asked, obviously horrified. "Those are the very places we should be *avoiding*."

"But if you were a hungry dog, where would you go?"

Miss Polley's face fell in chagrined acceptance, and she pushed her glasses back up her nose. Matthew had a hard time picturing her wrangling a stray dog. "I suppose you are right. But where are we going to find a butcher?"

"I can help with that," Matthew said, stepping forward. "Follow me."

He could only hope that they could take care of this discreetly enough that no one would notice what they were doing – and that Juliana and Miss Polley could avoid telling the butcher shop exactly what they thought of its practices.

For that had the potential to send this entire plan down a path that would be detrimental for all of them.

Matthew couldn't help but admire Juliana's bravery. Here was the daughter – now sister – of a duke, walking into a situation where she had no idea what to expect. The least he could do was to make sure that no one, be it human or canine, took advantage of her.

Matthew no longer followed behind as Juliana took to the alley beyond the butcher shop.

She had been right. There was a pack of four dogs currently fighting over a carcass of a type that Matthew couldn't actually recognize – and it looked like their quarrel was about to get ugly.

While he had been watching them, he had missed Juliana beginning to rush toward them, likely to stop them – but he had a feeling that she was only going to make things worse.

"Juliana!" he called out, racing after her, which of course alerted the dogs to their presence. One lifted its head and began to growl at them, and Juliana stopped her already slowed stride, which allowed Matthew to catch up to her. He placed a hand on her arm to halt her progress.

"Careful," he said, and when she nodded her understanding, he realized that she had already been slowing down, knowing how to approach the situation.

THE SECRET OF THE DASHING DETECTIVE

"We should go," he added, but she shook her head.

"Look at that one – it's limping," she said, pointing. "And the brown and white one has obviously been in an altercation of some kind."

She reached into the bag she carried and pulled out scraps, which began to alert the dogs, who lifted their heads and sniffed the air. Matthew held his hand out. "Let me," he said, and she opened her mouth to argue but he eyed her with a look that told her he would not listen to dissent in this.

"Let me, Juliana," he repeated. "Then we can accomplish your goal without me having to come rescue you."

"Fine, you can take the food," she said. "But I am walking with you."

"Very well."

She did, at least, stay one step behind him as he neared the dogs. The two that had been fighting over the bones neared him with interest while the other two hung back much more timidly. Matthew placed scraps in both hands and held them out to the two braver dogs, who had begun to inch forward.

"You're right," he murmured to Juliana. "This guy over here – the black one – has something wrong with his leg."

"I will try to put a splint on it," she said. "Mr. Livingstone showed us how."

Matthew didn't question what a human surgeon would know about treating a dog, but he supposed the man would know more than most other people would.

"Keep feeding him," Juliana whispered in his ear as she reached out and tentatively stroked the dog. The dog eyed her with some distrust but didn't back away.

She leaned in and placed the splint next to his leg before she began wrapping the bandage around it. The dog flinched and Matthew was ready to step between him and Juliana, but it didn't make any move to attack her.

"There," Juliana said after what seemed like an eternity but was actually only a few moments. "Finished."

She sat back on her heels, obviously pleased with her efforts. The dog looked down and immediately tried to eat the bandage.

"No, don't do that!" Juliana exclaimed, but before she could do anything more, the dog trotted away, likely to work at the bandage some more until he had successfully removed it.

The other dog sat there and stared at them as though waiting for more food. He had obviously been through a fair bit in his time, and before Matthew could stop her, Juliana was kneeling beside him and stroking his head.

"You're a pretty one, aren't you?" she crooned to the dog who could be called many things, but pretty was not one word that Matthew would use to describe him.

"You might do well to come with us to Father Abbot's sanctuary. What do you think?"

"What if he belongs to someone?" Matthew asked, but immediately regretted the question at the look Juliana shot him.

"If he does belong to someone, then they are obviously not taking good enough care of him to deserve to keep him. He looks as though he has been used as a fighting dog."

That seemed to decide it for her.

She slipped the rope around the dog's neck, and everyone was surprised when the dog obediently walked behind as though he understood that this was the best route for him to take.

Matthew could only follow behind them, ready to jump in if needed.

But it seemed in this, Juliana could fend for herself.

CHAPTER 12

"I'd say that was quite a successful day," Juliana said, her hands on her hips as she surveyed the dogs who were currently loaded in the back of the wagon Father Abbot had brought with him to transport the dogs to his sanctuary.

So far, none of them had turned on one another – people or canines – and she was hoping it remained that way.

She was somewhat reassured by Matthew, who stood at her back, keeping a wary, watchful eye out for anyone who might object to them taking a dog that was considered his or her own, but so far, they remained unchallenged. She knew he was worried and appreciated that he had come along and not only hadn't tried to force her to put a stop to this but had been there to support what she was trying to do.

She still couldn't get Lucy out of her mind, but she would have to hope she would return tomorrow.

They had just said their farewells to the rest of the group and were about to wave to James to come round in the carriage when they heard Matthew's name being called out.

"Mr. Archibald? Is that you?"

A true grin broke out on Juliana's face when she saw that the voice belonged to none other than Dr. Lewis, who was approaching them from down the street.

He was alone, a bag in his hand, and Juliana assumed that he had been working.

"Doctor," Matthew said, reaching out a hand and shaking it once they neared. Juliana had a feeling that he enjoyed her half-brother's company as much as she did, although he would refuse to allow himself to remove the barrier and become actual friends with the man – not when he still considered him a suspect in her abduction, her father's murder, and Giles' attempted murder. "How are you today?"

"Just fine," Dr. Lewis said. "All turned out well on my last house call and I am finished for the day. I'm returning home now. How are you doing, Mrs. Archibald?"

It took Juliana a moment to remember that *she* was Mrs. Archibald, and then she recalled why the doctor would be asking after her health. She swallowed and tried to recall what her symptoms were supposed to be.

"I am feeling slightly better," she managed. "Perhaps a bit nauseous."

"Ah yes, that is to be expected until you are slightly further along," he said. "If you ever would like to come see me, you just need to call me. In fact, I am on my way back and have some time if there is anything you would like to discuss?"

"No, no, I am fine," Juliana said, reaching out and gripping Matthew's hand in a desperate plea for him to help her out of this situation. She could *not* have her half-brother examine her, only to find that she was lying this entire time.

"That is good to hear," he said. "If you are returning to Holborn and have a moment, you could stop in with me and I could at least provide you with the names of midwives I would most trust, if you'd like."

"We would appreciate that," Matthew said smoothly. "We would be glad to accompany you."

Juliana looked at him, trying to signal that they would somehow have to get word to James and Abigail, who had remained in the carriage with her book and an extra shilling. Juliana hadn't needed Abigail following her when she would likely only be one more person for Matthew to watch over.

"If you will give us one moment, we must go say our farewells to a friend and then we would be happy to join you," Matthew said, tugging on Juliana's hand to have her follow him, and she looked up at him with some question.

"Why didn't you let me stay with him while you spoke to James?" she asked in a low voice. "I would have enjoyed some time to get to know him better."

"Because," Matthew said firmly, "I don't trust leaving you with anyone else. Especially when that man could have been the one who took you last time."

"I highly doubt that Dr. Lewis was the one who did so."

"So do I, if I am being honest," Matthew admitted. "But that doesn't change the fact that we cannot loosen our guard. We have to be careful."

"Very well," Juliana said as they approached the carriage on the side away from Dr. Lewis. Matthew told James their plan and asked him to follow along behind them at a distance, telling him that they would meet him a short distance away from Dr. Lewis' offices in Holborn. James nodded, used to Juliana's changing plans, and waited a moment to allow them time to make their way down the street with Dr. Lewis.

"Did you just finish dining?" he asked them as they approached, and Juliana and Matthew exchanged a look of confusion before she shook her head.

"No," Matthew said, "why do you ask?"

"This may sound odd," he said, "but you smell an awful lot

like smoked meat. Does the aroma not currently bother you, Mrs. Archibald?"

Juliana couldn't help but admit to herself that she was rather getting used to being referred to as Mrs. Archibald.

"It does, actually," she said, "but we were feeding some stray dogs and they certainly enjoyed it."

"I see," he said, although the slight tilt of his head told them that he didn't exactly understand, but that was fine – most people didn't understand it, at least not until they saw what her society did and learned more about it themselves. Like Matthew had, Juliana thought with a small smile.

The walk went by rather quickly with Dr. Lewis' company, and Juliana found herself more and more enjoying being in his presence. She could only hope that if he ever found out they had deceived him – and she supposed that he would have to if they were ever to have the relationship she hoped for – that he wouldn't forever hold it against them.

When they reached his home, she wasn't surprised to find that it was neat, orderly, and well-kept in a row of rather respectable looking townhouses in brown-brick.

"Here we are," Dr. Lewis said as he let them in the door and they stood in the front, where Juliana assumed patients usually waited. "I have a study in the back. I shall go write out these names for you and will be back shortly."

He returned after a couple of minutes and passed Juliana the list – which made her more impressed with him than she had even been before. Most men would always defer to the husband, or the brother, or the father. But this new half-brother of hers treated her as if she was a person in her own right, and she appreciated it more than he could know.

"Thank you," she said with a wide smile. "Thank you very much."

He nodded. "Of course." He paused a moment, rocking

back and forth from his heels to his toes as though considering something before he spoke.

"I know it is a rather odd request, considering we just met, and I do not have a wife myself, but if you would ever like to dine together again, it would be a pleasure to do so. It's strange, but I feel as though we have known each other for quite some time."

Juliana reached out a hand and laid it on his arm. "I completely understand," she said. "And we would be happy to invite you over for an evening."

Dr. Lewis beamed back at her until Matthew cleared his throat from behind her and Juliana immediately felt the blood rushing from her face as she realized that she had lost herself in the moment and her enthusiasm in getting to know her brother. For to Dr. Lewis, she and Matthew were married, and certainly would not be living in the middle of Mayfair in one of London's largest mansions.

"Have a good evening, Dr. Lewis," Matthew said before steering Juliana out the door, the note clutched in her hand, and they made their farewells before they stepped out into the slowly cooling late afternoon air.

Matthew looked over at her and began to shake his head. "I believe you will ever surprise me."

"I know that was stupid," she said, instantly chagrined. "It just came out of my mouth before I realized that you and I can hardly entertain together, especially at Warwick House." She paused as a thought came over her. "Perhaps we can ask him to dinner one night at your home?"

Matthew was already shaking his head. "Absolutely not."

"Why not?"

"I live by myself in a boarding house apartment. Most of the other occupants are also single men. It would be quite odd for the two of us to live in one, especially if we are expecting a child. And there is clearly no sign a woman lives with me."

Juliana was actually rather glad to hear that, but she wasn't about to say it aloud.

"I shall have to see it some time and consider it for myself. We could always tell him that we are about to move."

"Juliana—"

But James approached them at that point, halting their conversation. He looked rather weary as he asked, "Home, my lady?" and she nodded. They all deserved to be finished with this day, and most certainly would require something to eat.

"Home, James," she said, as Matthew took his seat away from her – reminding her that this was all just a game, as much as she wanted it to be true.

* * *

THEY WERE NEARING Mayfair when Matthew heard his name being called out again, and he looked around, wondering just who had tracked him down now – another one of his family members, or a suspect again?

But there was no one in sight. Then he heard the voice again and he told James to slow slightly.

"Matthew?" Juliana said from within. "I believe someone is calling for you."

"Yes, I heard it," he said in a low voice, even as all of the hair on his body seemed to stand on end. Something wasn't right. The night sky had begun to descend upon them, and they were just about to leave Holborn. There were far too many dark alleyways for him to properly see within them. He would prefer they continue on their way.

"Keep on, James," he said, as his name was called again –

there was no denying it – only this time there was a "help!" added to the end of it.

Matthew was at war within himself. They were in Holborn. It could be someone from his family, or if not, an old friend. But he had no desire to leave Juliana and knew that it could be foolish to do so.

"James, can you drive near the alleyway where the voice is coming from? But be sure not to stop."

James nodded, beginning to steer the carriage toward where Matthew pointed. As they neared, the sound came again, closer this time.

Matthew jumped down from the carriage as it still moved.

"Keep driving, James," he said, one of his hands on the side as he tried to see through the darkness.

As the carriage slowed, however, he suddenly heard Juliana from the other side.

"Matthew, help!"

He rounded the back of the carriage faster than he had ever moved before, in time to see a man, a cap pulled tightly over his face, trying to force his way in through the carriage door. He was having difficulty, however, as Juliana was bashing him over the head with a large beef bone that had been leftover from the day, one she had been planning on giving to Lucy.

"Get away!" she shouted again and, as Matthew began to charge toward him, the man finally gave up and ran away.

Matthew had nearly lost his breath – something that rarely happened – when he reached Juliana.

"Are you all right?" he asked, wrenching open the carriage door and running his hands over her arms.

"I'm fine," she said between quick breaths. "Are you?"

"Yes," he said as he realized how bad this could have been.

"But we have to get out of here. This was a trap – that much is certain."

"I agree," she said, and he didn't care then whether Abigail was watching, or James, or if even the bloody duke himself had an eye on them. He leaned in and gave Juliana a hard, quick kiss on the lips, just to show her how glad he was that she was alive, unwell, and unharmed.

He leaned back to find her watching him with wide eyes, and he managed a small smile as he jumped back up with James and told him to go – and go fast.

He had nearly been taken advantage of. Someone wanted him to leave Juliana alone so that they could access her without him there.

Which was one thing he vowed, with new resolution, that he would never allow to happen again.

CHAPTER 13

Juliana slept fitfully, convinced in her dreams that she was being chased.

Which made sense when she considered that her pursuer had come close once more, and that she already knew what it was like to be entirely at the mercy of a stranger who most certainly did not have her best interests at heart.

It was not the first time such nightmares had overwhelmed her, but tonight, at the point in her dream when she became so desperate that she nearly woke up, she was overwhelmed by something else – another presence, one who stepped in at the last moment and led her to safety.

Matthew.

He was there to make sure that she was never alone, that she always had an escape. She clung to that, until thinking of him caused her dreams to change entirely, and she was nearly frantic with needing him to be there with her in the moment, to wrap his arms around her – only not to keep her safe, but to push her to the edge of what she knew as comfort.

It was quite the conundrum.

When the morning sun peered through the curtains until Abigail pulled them back fully, flooding the room with light, Juliana decided that she would feel better if she went to feed Lucy, that seeing her again would bring her some joy and normality. Only, when she and Emma went to the fence an hour later, she found all the dogs there *except* Lucy. Juliana had no idea if something had happened to the dog, or if Lucy had decided that yesterday had been too much for her to return, but Juliana missed her.

"What's wrong?" Emma asked from where she stood behind her, the sun reflecting on the blond in her hair. She must have caught Juliana's mood this morning, for she had insisted on accompanying her on this morning visit. It was strange. In the entirety of her life, Juliana had spent more time with Emma than nearly any other person – until Emma had moved into the same house as her. Now when they actually lived together, she saw her much less frequently, for Emma spent so much of her time with Giles.

Which was fine. They were newlyweds, and already sharing their time – and their home – with the rest of their family.

"Lucy isn't here," Juliana said dejectedly as she fed the other dogs. "I'm afraid she might have been scared away."

"She'll be back," Emma said, placing a comforting hand on Juliana's shoulder before they turned and started back toward the house.

"How are you enjoying your new role as duchess?" Juliana asked, changing the subject, and Emma bit her lip in some uncertainty.

"I am happy to be Giles' wife," she said, "and I always knew that if I married, I would likely be the wife of a peer. I just never expected it to be a role of such a high status. It is rather intimidating."

"Especially with my mother watching over your shoulder," Juliana couldn't help but add with a snort, to which Emma laughed.

"This is true," she said carefully. "Although I will say she has been quite respectful, for the most part, and has already offered to move into the dowager house when we return to the countryside. As for here in London, Warwick House is so large that I cannot imagine the rest of you leaving for anywhere else. Why, Giles and I would hardly even need the servants anymore!"

"I suppose that works as long as my mother doesn't interfere with your role," Juliana said. They had always jested before about how awful her mother would make life for the woman Giles would one day marry. They just hadn't, of course, ever considered that it might actually be Emma. It was not that Juliana's mother didn't mean well – it was just that she had her own idea of the right way to do things and she wasn't afraid to share her opinions.

"How are you enjoying your time with Mr. Archibald?" Emma asked, eyeing her knowingly, and Juliana's mouth dropped open for a moment before she snapped it closed again.

"I suppose I can say that it has not been the hardship I assumed it would be. He has been respectful in terms of watching me from a distance."

"But do you enjoy distance between you?"

"Emma!"

"I am sorry, Jules, but it is rather obvious that the two of you have eyes for one another."

Juliana paused for a moment as she tried to determine whether she should continue to pretend that there was nothing between her and Matthew or if she should admit all, but her long friendship with Emma won out. Once she made the decision to share, it all began pouring out, and she could feel her entire body practically lighting up with the excitement of the closeness she was sharing with Matthew.

"Oh, Emma, he is... well he is everything I never realized that I wanted in a man. I know I always said that I would marry a man who could provide for me and allow me to live the life I wanted without any restrictions, but... then I came to know Matthew. Whatever is between us is so much more than that. There is this attraction between us that I just cannot deny."

"A spark?"

"A *flame*," Juliana said. "When we kiss – which has only been a couple of times now – it is like nothing else in the world matters but me and him and that moment. It is difficult to explain."

"You don't have to explain," Emma said with a small smile. "I already know."

Juliana supposed that if this is what Emma felt like when she was with Giles, then she couldn't begrudge her friend for marrying her brother.

Which was the moment when she realized that she *did* slightly begrudge Emma for it. She didn't want to – not at all – but their friendship had changed, and, in a way, Juliana felt left behind.

She wondered if Emma felt the change too, and when Juliana looked up and met her gaze, she realized that she did.

Of course she did. This was Emma, the woman with whom she had been inseparable since they were children.

"Emma," she said, feeling instantly regretful, "I am sorry—"

Emma was already waving away her words. "You have nothing to apologize for."

"I know, but—"

"You were never anything but supportive of me and Giles

together, Jules, even though I know it must have been difficult for you to see us together."

"I wouldn't say it was *difficult*," Juliana said, clasping her hands together as they walked the long way around the hedgerow, both aware that they needed time to speak of this. "It was just... odd."

"It was odd for me too," Emma said. "But I also had Giles. I didn't spend enough time considering your feelings."

Juliana turned to her and took her hands in hers. "Let's put it behind us, shall we? I know our friendship will never be exactly the same as it once was. But that doesn't mean it has to be better or worse – just different."

Emma smiled with undisguised joy. "That sounds wonderful to me."

They leaned in and hugged one another, just as they heard a slight yapping from the fence. Juliana broke away to look out and see Lucy sitting on the other side of the fence.

"There you are," she said, walking over to the bars and crouching down. She reached into her bag for the bone she had saved – the one that she bashed over the head of the man who tried to enter her carriage. "Here you go, girl."

As the dog ran off with the bone, Juliana stood and eyed Emma with a small smile.

"Now, do I have a story for you."

* * *

MATTHEW WASN'T sure whether this was one of his better ideas or one of his lesser ones.

He had been putting off teaching Juliana how to protect herself for long enough – because he wasn't certain that he could trust himself to be in such close proximity to her once again.

Which proved over again why he shouldn't be allowing himself to come so close – because it put his own basic desires above what was best for her, what would lead to safety for their entire family, and would allow him to do his job to the best of his ability.

He had come to the point where he had considered asking Owen to take over his role, but in the end, he found that he couldn't even trust his closest of friends and the most reliable man he knew with Juliana.

For there was no one else in this world he would put in charge of her care —no one but himself.

When Matthew entered the house, Jamison led him through a maze of rooms, telling him that she was conversing with the new duchess, until they reached one of the parlors – how many parlors were in this house anyway? The two women had their heads together, laughing over something that appeared to be needlework, and Juliana seemed surprised to see him, for he hadn't told her that he was planning on visiting today. When he explained his reason for being there, she seemed a mixture of hesitant and determined.

"I thought we already practiced how to protect myself," she said, her brow furrowing, and he shook his head.

"We practiced what to do when you are attacked from behind. Now you need to learn what to do when challenged."

"Very well," she said. "I know just the place to practice."

She stood and crossed the room to the door, stopping when she reached it, looking back at the duchess.

"Would you like to come, Emma?" Juliana asked, but the duchess waved her hand at them.

"No, you go on ahead," she said, with a look on her face that Matthew would call knowing. "Have fun."

She gave a little wiggle of one of her eyebrows that had

Juliana half-choking, half-laughing before she hurried him out of the room.

"You seem to be on good terms with your brother's wife," he noted as she led him down the hall toward whatever room this was that she had deemed as most appropriate for their purposes.

"With Emma?" Juliana said with wide eyes. "We have been the best of friends since we were children!"

"I knew you were friends. I just hadn't been sure of how close of friends you remained since she married your brother."

"To be honest, the time following the wedding was more difficult than I had thought it would be," Juliana admitted, and he slowed his steps slightly to match hers as they moved side-by-side down the hall. "Emma and I have been friends for as long as I can remember and then, suddenly, she's Giles' wife. I do enjoy having her closer than ever – physically – but things are different now. I believe we've come to an understanding, however."

She smiled so brightly at that that it lit his own heart.

"Was Lucy happy to see you this morning?" he asked, wanting to see more happiness from her.

"She was," Juliana said, her smile spreading. "At first, I was worried when she wasn't with the other dogs where I normally meet them. But as Emma and I returned to the house, she showed up along the fence. She was quite taken with my weapon."

"Your weapon?"

"The dog bone I used on our culprit last night."

"Ah, that one," he said, his cheer fading. "Speaking of weapons, that's part of what I wanted to practice today."

"Weapons?"

He nodded. "I won't give you a pistol for fear that you would shoot yourself—"

She seemed prepared with a retort at that, but he forged ahead before she could say anything.

"—but I do think you should carry a knife. Just in case."

"A *knife?*" Juliana raised an eyebrow. "I'm not sure that I could ever actually use it on someone."

"And if I have anything to do with it, you won't have to. But I would feel better knowing that you have something to defend yourself with, or at least to threaten someone with if ever required."

"I have no idea how to use a knife."

"Which is why I'm here – to teach you."

Juliana had shown him through so many rooms and corridors that Matthew was beginning to feel rather dizzy. He was always a man who kept close track of his circumstances and location as possible, but he wasn't entirely sure that he would be able to find his way out if Juliana left him behind.

She finally stopped in front of a door, which opened as soon as they stopped in front of it.

"Oh!" Lady Prudence stepped back in surprise, her hair mussed around her face, in a strange garment that he supposed could be described as a dress but seemed much looser than most. "I just finished."

"Do you mind if we use the room?" Juliana asked, although she was already pushing past Prudence as though her response didn't entirely matter.

"Of course," Lady Prudence said, following them in. "What for?"

"Matthew is, apparently, going to teach me how to use a knife," Juliana said as she walked toward the center of the room while Matthew stopped and stared.

The room looked like Angelo's Fencing Academy, a place he had been to once before upon invitation from a friend, but it was even more tidy and organized. The walls were covered in navy blue fabric, while skylights at the top of the room allowed light to enter, leaving crisscrossed patterns on the floor. Along one wall was specialized wooden shelving holding a number of swords of various heights – although most were for those of a person of rather short stature.

"If you wanted to learn to use a sword, you know I could have taught you," Lady Prudence said, her hands on her hips.

"A sword is much different than a knife," Juliana said, although Matthew doubted she knew much on the subject. It seemed Lady Prudence, however, was something of an expert.

"Perhaps, but some of the principles are the same, are they not?" Lady Prudence said, this time her words directed at Matthew, who shrugged.

"I suppose so," he said, "although most fencing I have partaken in is for sport. Fighting with a knife… is for other purposes entirely."

"That is true," Lady Prudence said, although she had a look to her that made Matthew suspect that she had perhaps seen more than she would ever admit. She paused as though wondering whether or not she should stay, but then finally she seemed to make up her mind and started for the door. "Perhaps we shall have to spar later, Jules."

And with her glib farewell, Matthew and Juliana were left alone.

Matthew placed a bag on the floor, unfastened the clasps, and pulled out a sheathed knife. He took it from its case, grasped the blade end of it in his hand and held it out to Juliana.

"For you, my lady," he said with a small smile and mock bow.

She took it with the same approach she had kissing him – little expertise but enough enthusiasm to make up for it.

She held it up by the hilt with enough of a thrust forward to have him stepping backward a bit.

She grinned at his response before placing a hand on her hip.

"Well?" she said, "shall we get started?"

CHAPTER 14

Juliana was teasing him on purpose – mostly to distract herself from her nerves.

Nerves from spending time alone with Matthew (she prayed Prudence wouldn't say anything to their mother), and nerves at the fact that he was teaching her how to use a weapon.

If anyone had told her a short time ago that she would be wielding a knife with the intention of possibly using it on a person one day, she would have laughed in his or her face.

Added to that was the fact that the very man teaching her the skills was one she couldn't stop dreaming about, and she was in a world of trouble.

She watched with interest as he walked to the center of the room, where Prudence practiced her daily fencing regime. Juliana's sister had taken up the skill as a child after watching their brother, Giles, learn the sport from their father, who had been infatuated with fencing. But when Giles had left them, Prudence had continued on without him.

Juliana could never understand why her father had allowed Prudence to take part, but then, he was such a fanatic for the sport that she imagined he was happy to have some kind of connection to it, someone to pass down his love for it to, as Giles refused to have anything to do with him or activities he enjoyed.

The sun glinted off Matthew's cheekbones, pulling Juliana from her reminiscing as she couldn't focus on anything but Matthew's magnificence. She had acknowledged how handsome he was the first time she had seen him – they had all commented upon it – but it wasn't until more recently that she truly appreciated how striking he was.

"So tell me," she said, feigning nonchalance as she strolled over to where he stood in the center of the sunshine, "how do you plan to teach me such a sport?"

"It's not a sport," he said gruffly as he knelt and reached back into the bag. "This is a game of life or death, Juliana."

The seriousness of his words sobered her, and she stopped teasing and waited. When he stood, he was holding pieces of fabric with pins that he placed on his chest and in the center of his abdomen.

"These are targets," he said, and then reached out and used his hands to grasp her shoulders and move her into position. When he finished arranging the two of them, he was standing about half a length away from her – much farther than she would have liked.

"Shouldn't we be closer?" she asked, wrinkling her nose at him, and he shook his head.

"Not yet. Proximity is of the utmost importance in a knife fight," he explained. "Now, the first thing to understand is what to do if someone comes at you with a weapon." He lifted the back of his jacket and pulled out a sheathed knife of his own, lifting it between them. "If you can, take the option to run."

"To run?"

How was that helpful in teaching her skills?

"Run," he nodded. "While I will give you some tricks in defending yourself, you will never be as proficient as someone who has trained – or who has used a knife for such purposes before and has no issues in using it again. If you can, you run and find help as quickly as you can."

"And if that is not an option?"

"Hold your weapon up like this," he instructed, and then stepped in and moved her fingers into the proper position. Heat practically shimmered out from where their skin touched. "Then stay back about this distance. If you get any closer, it turns into a boxing match which you must avoid at all costs when holding weapons."

She nodded, understanding what he said even as a tremor ran through her at the thought that it was actually possible she might be found in such a situation.

"You don't have the killing instinct – in fact I could hardly imagine that you could be any further from a woman with a killing instinct," he said with a slight snort, and she stopped and tilted her head.

"Are you making fun of me?"

"No." The corners of his lips quirked.

"There is nothing for me to be embarrassed about. I am glad that I am able to help animals who have no one else or who are being treated inhumanely."

"And I commend you for it," he said, leaning into her so that she could see the crystal blue of his eyes. "But it doesn't make you the contender I would bet on in a knife fight."

"I suppose that's fair," she acknowledged.

"What you need to do is focus on trying to connect with the attacker's knife hand."

"Why?"

"If you can slice through tendons or muscle, then he would have no choice but to drop the knife and you will then be *free* to run."

She shivered at the thought but nodded resolutely and allowed him to continue. She would not be left to face another situation like she had previously.

"Very well," she said. "How do I do that?"

"I will show you the how, but more important is the when."

"When?"

"You need to work on timing your strike. You must strike just before, just after, or *as* the attacker is lashing out at you. If your timing is accurate, you will catch him off guard and be able to make your mark."

"And as for *how* to strike?"

"It's in your wrist," he said. "Here, let me show you."

He placed his own knife on the floor and moved so that he was standing behind her. She tilted her head back slightly into him, enjoying his closeness, and she had to physically stop herself from snuggling her body in closer to him where the rough material of his jacket brushed against her back.

His strong fingers wrapped around her wrist as he pulled her arm back, then stretched it forward.

"This is a jabbing motion," he said, teaching her to move her wrist as though she was throwing a punch.

"Then you have the slice," he continued, taking her hand in his, and running it from one side to the other in a smooth motion. Juliana's breath caught.

"And finally, we have the upward stab," he said, thrusting her hand, wrapped around the knife, upward before them. "I— I am not sure you'll be needing that one," he said, and she was pleased to see that he was apparently just as affected as she was.

"Let's hope not," she murmured, unable to fathom the thought.

"Try them all a few times – go through them one at a time," he said, stepping back away from her and she immediately missed the loss of his presence at her back, so solid and comforting and... *necessary*.

It scared her with its strength, that she could so badly want a man she knew she could never have.

But in the meantime, she would enjoy this time with him. Even if it could only lead to heartbreak.

She reached out a hand to touch him before he moved too far, but he shook it off gently, causing her to warm in embarrassment. While Juliana longed to be close to this man, she realized that he knew what it meant to have family and love and passion – and was likely much more aware of what was at stake between them.

Juliana reminded herself that he was surely much more experienced than she, that he knew better, and she should defer to his wishes. And yet, even though she had been raised to do as she was told — with authority to come from her father and then her brother or husband – whichever came first – it wasn't in her nature to follow along. She knew that she was an oddity, that any other young woman of the *ton* would think her mad not to do as was expected of her. But what was she to do with this man before her, so tempting as a treasure at the end of a map without clear direction until now?

The man on her mind was currently walking away from her, however, toward the bag. She couldn't help her curiosity at what else could be hiding in there.

"Is that... paint?"

He nodded. "You are going to practice with a paint brush as you cannot very well practice with a knife. You need to try to hit the targets. We'll see how close you get."

"I cannot paint your clothes!" she exclaimed.

"Then be sure to hit the pieces of fabric," he said with a quick grin, and she crossed her arms.

"We know that will not happen easily. I'm afraid I have never been particularly gifted with skills such as accuracy."

"I will wash the jacket if needed."

She knew how much such a garment would be worth.

"I cannot ruin it. I will not."

"This is important."

"No."

"Very well," he said, apparently having decided not to argue with her stubbornness as he made up his mind about something. "You can paint my skin."

And that's when he started to undo his jacket.

Juliana knew what she *should* do. She should tell him to stop, that if they were caught, this would make her already suspect reputation irreparable.

But Matthew, apparently, felt ensuring her safety was more important than her reputation, as he didn't seem inclined to stop.

Juliana didn't have it within her to force the issue, and all she could do was stand there and watch with growing desire as he shed one layer after another.

His jacket slipped off his shoulders and dropped to the floor.

His fingers came to his cravat and tugged it free before it followed suit and he began to twist each button of his shirt through their holes before he lifted the shirt over his head, revealing a spectacularly sculpted torso that made Juliana's mouth water. She had to snap it shut to keep from appearing like one of the fish in the fountain at their country estate.

Matthew, however, didn't seem to realize how flustered she was. When Juliana gathered herself, she noticed a small, puckered scar beneath his left chest muscle, and she couldn't stop herself from stepping forward and running her finger along it. His head snapped up and his gaze met hers.

"What are you—"

THE SECRET OF THE DASHING DETECTIVE

"Where is this from?"

He closed his eyes for a few seconds, seemingly resigned to answer her question. "I was on a case and the suspect wasn't entirely thrilled about being followed. He caught me unaware."

"I see," she said, but she didn't lift her finger away from the scar. Instead, she allowed it to slide along his chest to the center, where she wrapped one of his whorls of hair around her finger.

The rise and fall of his chest increased in speed, and she heard the hitch in his throat.

"Juliana," he murmured, his voice hoarse as he reached in and wrapped his hand around her finger.

She placed the entire palm of her hand over his chest for just a moment, feeling the beat of his heart, so strong and powerful beneath her fingers, before she stepped back and away from him, stopping herself before she did anything truly foolish.

He turned and reached into the apparently bottomless bag and pulled out a paintbrush as well as a bottle of blue paint and a tray. He mixed the paint and dipped the brush in it before standing and holding out the handle of the brush to her.

"Here."

"Is this your paint?" she asked as she took it, thinking of the magnificent drawings he had provided her.

"Yes. I used to enjoy the hobby."

"But you don't anymore."

"No."

"Why not?"

"I don't have the time. Now, enough questions, Juliana. We must begin."

She took pity on him and respected his wishes, taking a step back. He placed himself the same distance away from her as he had been before. His knife was in its sheath as he held it out in front of him.

"Pretend I am attacking," he said. "I will not attempt to strike you – not even with it sheathed – but it will give you an idea of the timing. You have choices. Sometimes you have to do what is available to you. Aim for my hand if you prefer but if you cannot, then be sure to hit one of the strike zones I showed you – heart or stomach."

"I—"

"It's a paintbrush. Remember that for now."

She nodded, even though she couldn't rid herself of the thought that, at some point, it might not be a paintbrush any longer.

She tried to remember everything he taught her as he lunged toward her and a second later, she reached in to try to paint his hand, but he was too quick for her.

He stepped back and studied her for a moment before nodding his head abruptly as he seemed to make up his mind about something.

"Your footwork is messy."

"Pardon me?"

"You lunged toward me with too big of a step. It put you off balance and I could have easily knocked you over or, as I did, evade your attempt. Think of dancing – you dance, yes?"

"Of course."

"Take small, precise steps – one, two, three – but quickly, so that you maintain your balance but take the person off guard. Practice for me."

She nodded and did as he said. One-two-three, she counted, moving much more quickly across the floor. He was right.

"Try again," he said, and positioned himself across from her. He made his advance and just before he was able to

THE SECRET OF THE DASHING DETECTIVE

reach his knife toward her, she painted him right across the chest.

He nodded with a grim smile. "Good. Again."

They practiced the steps, over and over, Matthew relentless in having her repeat the movements until her legs were tired and her arm was on fire and a bead of sweat broke out along her brow.

Matthew finally must have realized her fatigue as he nodded and said, "That's good enough for now."

He reached down, about to pick up his clothing, but Juliana stepped in close to him before he could do so. She had spent so much time wondering about him, about what was growing between them, and while she knew he was trying to avoid it, she couldn't help but want to pursue it further.

"Matthew," she said, her voice breathless as she replaced her hand on his chest, where she had last touched him and had decided she wasn't finished yet. "Don't get dressed yet."

"Why not?"

"I've just... I've never seen a man like you."

"Have you seen many men?" he asked, a hint of teasing in his voice, and she laughed back at him.

"No, actually, I have not."

"Good," he said, his voice so solid, with such possessiveness that a surge of triumph rushed through her.

She ran her hands up and over his chest, exploring the tautness of his muscle and the solidity of his collarbones before she continued down, over the lines of paint she had left on him to the indents separating his stomach muscles. She moved then lower, and lower still, until she reached the waistband of his pants – but he didn't allow her any farther.

"Juliana," he muttered hoarsely, wrapping his hands around her wrists. "You have to stop."

"Why?"

"Because."

But that wasn't enough of an explanation for her. So instead of continuing this talk, she did what she had been longing to do since the last time they had been so close together – she stood on her toes and brought her lips up to his.

She pressed her lips against him, not sure whether she was asking or taking, but it seemed he didn't have quite enough restraint to hold out against her and after a moment of hesitation, she felt him give in, his lips beginning to move, more slowly this time, as they explored one another and all they had to offer each other. A warm glow of pleasure began to move through Juliana, from where they touched down through her body to the very bottom of her toes and she melted into him, her arms reaching up to curl around his neck.

He pulled her in close, as she was ready to give him anything he wanted or asked of her as his tongue slipped into her mouth and stroked against hers in an intimate love play that had her shivering against him.

Juliana closed her eyes as the sun caressed her face and this man, her protector, her near-lover, caressed her body, her mouth, her soul.

Until finally he eased back away from her, although he didn't go far as he rested his forehead against hers and they stood there together, swaying back and forth in a dance unlike any other.

CHAPTER 15

"Matthew, that was—"

He placed a finger against her lips. He couldn't hear her say how wonderful it was, how it seemed meant to be, how she couldn't wait to do it again.

For they couldn't. He had to cease this before it went any further, as much as it nearly destroyed him to have to do so.

"Juliana, I'm sorry, but this... this cannot happen again."

She pushed back away from him, far enough so that she was looking up at him, the green in her eyes intensified by desire and now dismay. "I believe I have heard that before. Whyever not?"

He sighed although he couldn't stop himself from running his hands through the tendrils of her hair that had slipped out of its elegant designs during their practice.

"You know why, Juliana. I am not the man for you. I am not good enough for you. I shouldn't even be touching you, let alone—"

Let alone envisioning a life with her. For that was what was going through his mind, although he didn't want to put words to it, didn't want to voice it aloud, and certainly did not want to tell her. For their lives could never be one. They were from different worlds that didn't belong together.

"Matthew," she said, reaching up and stroking his face with her soft, cool, hands. "Do not say such a thing."

"It's the truth."

"It is not," she said so insistently that he nearly believed her as she emphatically shook her head at him. "You are the best man I have ever met. You care for others. You would do anything for me, and I cannot thank you enough for that. I feel things for you that I never even thought possible. I know that we cannot have a traditional courtship, but we can at least continue to spend time with one another, to see how much of this is real, can we not?"

They couldn't. It would only make things worse. He knew that, in the back of his mind, and yet he couldn't stand the thought of not being with her. If this is was all they would ever have, then damn it, he would take it, as imprudent as he was for doing so.

"Very well," he said. "Although your brother will have my hide if he ever finds out."

"Then we won't let him," she said with an impish grin that he knew was going to get them both in trouble.

"Juliana?"

They both started at a voice from out in the hall, and Matthew bent and donned his shirt as quickly as possible. He managed to dress rather quickly and respectably, missing only his cravat, before the knock sounded on the door and Lady Prudence peeked her head in. Her eyebrows rose at the scene before her, but she said nothing about it.

"Giles wants to see all of us. It seems that he and Mother have something they want to share."

Matthew nodded to the door. "Go," he said to Juliana. "I can see myself out."

"I believe Giles would like you to come as well, *Mr.*

Archibald," Lady Prudence said, emphasizing his name, obviously a reminder to Juliana as to who he should be to her.

When Lady Prudence returned to the hall, Matthew quickly packed up his bag and reached out, fixing Juliana's hair so that she looked closer to how she had when they had entered the room. "Very well. Let us go."

They followed Lady Prudence – who had changed into a different gown – out the door and down the stairs, back through the maze of rooms and corridors until they reached the front, formal drawing room. The tableau in front of them featured the duke standing on one side of the room, arms crossed with a dark look on his face, his wife by his side with one hand on his arm as though trying to calm him. Their mother sat in a chair in the middle of the room with an uncertain look on her face as though she was under inquisition, and Lady Winchester perched on the sofa, hands on her walking stick with her chin lifted upward in a self-righteous tilt.

"Please, sit," the duke said as they walked into the room. "My mother has something she would like to say to us all."

The dowager duchess bristled. "I really do not understand why this is of any importance."

"I told you to share this weeks ago, Elizabeth," Lady Winchester said smartly. "When you refused, I gave you the option – to tell Giles yourself, or I would do it for you. You made your choice. Now he knows."

"Tell us about Hudson Lewis, Mother," the duke said in a chilled voice, his words startling Matthew, who had taken up a place standing at the back of the room after Juliana and Lady Prudence had flanked their grandmother on the sofa.

"To be honest, I did not even know the man's name, for it hardly matters," she said with a shrug of her shoulders, as Matthew noticed Juliana lean in toward her mother, clearly having an opinion on the matter, although she said nothing yet.

"Mother," the duke warned tersely.

"Very well. I knew your father had been paying off a woman – a Mrs. Lewis – for years. Apparently he sired a child with her. He told me one night in the midst of one of his fits of anger, as if providing me the information would cause me some pain." She snorted. "I was just glad he found someone else to foist himself upon."

Juliana and Prudence looked at one another in shock as Juliana let out a cough that Matthew was sure was meant to hide the sound of her surprise at her mother's words.

"There was a child, and the woman threatened to make it known. I am not sure why it would have mattered – plenty of noblemen have by-blows wandering around. But your father decided that it would mar the reputation he felt was so pristine and he decided that instead he would pay her to keep mum about the situation."

"And look after the boy."

They all looked to Juliana, who had finally said her mind. She lifted a hand. "He was Father's son. He *should* have looked after him, financially if in no other way, should he not have?"

"Well, I—"

"It's true," Lady Prudence added in support of her sister. "It was his responsibility."

"That is not the way of things. However, as it were, the boy grew up, moved to London, and apparently your father stopped paying the woman when the boy had finished his education. That is all I know."

"Why didn't you tell us?" the duke insisted, and their mother looked at him in some horror.

"Why *would* I tell you? What difference does it make?"

"He's our brother," Juliana said, but her mother was already shaking her head.

"He is *not* your brother. Not in any way that matters."

"You're wrong," Juliana said quietly before she stood. "Is that all?"

"Is it, Mother?" the duke asked, and she nodded.

"You should have told us as soon as the family came under threat," the duke said, and the dowager duchess' eyes widened.

"You believe this man could be the one who is threatening us?"

"Likely not, but he *is* a suspect," Matthew said, finally speaking up, and all eyes turned toward him, as though they had forgotten that he was there. "He is one of the leads we are following up on."

"I am going to go walk about the gardens," Juliana said, apparently done with the conversation. "I shall return shortly."

"Do not go alone!" her mother called after her, and the duke looked over at Matthew who nodded in understanding and followed her out.

"Take Abigail!" the dowager duchess added at Matthew's accompaniment, and he heard Juliana sigh before she asked the butler to find her maid.

When the three of them were finally ready, Juliana walked out the front door, Matthew and the maid following dutifully behind. Once they were a distance away, Juliana stopped and turned around.

"Abigail, would you like to sit on the bench and look out over the water for a time?"

Abigail nodded as Juliana passed her a bag of sweets, which the girl took with great glee.

Matthew waited as they walked deeper through the

hedgerows, aware that Juliana obviously wanted to speak to him about what had just transpired.

"That was an interesting conversation," she noted, to which he nodded.

"It was, although I'm afraid that your mother did not impart any new information."

"No, she didn't, but she did prove something."

"Which is?"

Juliana turned to him now, placing her hands on his chest, and he looked around to make sure they were out of view of the house.

"My mother... she does what she thinks is best for us, but she is not entirely a good person. My father most certainly was not. I love my brother and my sister, and they have always been my world, but they are no better than anyone of lesser status. Neither am I trying and spectacularly failing to say is that you *think* you are not good enough for me, but that is not at all the truth. I have met your family and they are the most wonderful people. They may not be the family of a duke, but they have hearts that are worth more than any title. If you ask me – and I know you are not asking, but I will tell you regardless – I am the one who is not good enough for *you.*"

Her words melted something within him, something that had been holding him back.

"You would always be good enough for me, Juliana, but that doesn't change certain facts."

"Such as?"

"You and I would never be allowed to be together. Not by your mother or your brother—"

"Giles can be convinced. I just will not give him a choice."

"You are going to tell the duke what to do?"

"Do not underestimate my powers of persuasion," she

THE SECRET OF THE DASHING DETECTIVE

said with a wink, and somehow, he believed her. Look how far she had convinced him, after all.

She stood on her toes and looked up at him, not kissing him this time, but obviously waiting for him to make the first move.

With a sigh he lowered his mouth to hers, unable to resist her. She certainly knew how to make a compelling argument, and if she were a man he would suggest she become a barrister to argue her case – for he wasn't sure how anyone could ever deny her anything.

He thought of her work on the pamphlet, of the passion she felt for her society and her cause, and he acknowledged how lucky they all were to have her on their side.

And how fortunate he was to have a woman like her in his arms, on his lips, whether it was for now or forever.

He surrendered to her and to her kiss, and she leaned in closer to him. He couldn't help his hands from wandering around the back of her dress and up her sides until they were cupping her breasts, even as he knew he shouldn't touch her, but she dispelled all of his hesitancies.

"Yes," she breathed into him, and it was all the encouragement he needed to brush his thumbs over her nipples, which hardened at his touch. She arched into him, clearly enjoying it, and he slipped a hand into the bodice of her gown and found her soft skin. Her nipple pebbled even further, and she, likely unknowingly, ground herself against his aching erection as he cupped her and teased her. He left her mouth, his lips nipping her earlobe before tracing a line down her neck to her collarbone. He could only imagine what she would look like underneath him without a stitch of clothing, ready for his exploration. The thought nearly brought him to his knees, especially when it seemed she was ready to make it happen.

She reached for the fall of his trousers, and he wondered

if she even knew what she was searching for, but he broke away from her before it could go any further, his breathing heavy as he stared down at her swollen, pink lips and heaving chest.

"Juliana," he said desperately, and she leaned into him.

"I want more."

"We cannot."

"Maybe not now, not here," she said. "But at some point. I want—I *need* more."

"Do you even understand what that more is?"

"I have an idea," she said with an impish grin. "My grandmother provided me and Prudence with quite a few of the particulars."

Matthew nearly choked at that piece of information, especially at the thought of it coming from Lady Winchester.

"I'm not sure what to say to that."

"Say that we will – that we can."

"I cannot make any promises," he finally said. "I do not want to ruin you for... for whoever will one day become your husband."

She narrowed her eyes at him. "And just who do you suppose that will be?"

"You seemed fairly intent on Lord Hemingway."

She looked away from him, the breeze causing her stray hair to float away from her face. "I need to speak to him, actually," she said. "I have no wish to, for I will only be letting him down, which brings me no joy. But I also cannot marry him. We both know that."

Matthew reached out and took her hands in his. "If I am being honest, I must tell you that I have never felt for another woman the way I feel for you. But Juliana... how would we have a future together? What do I have to offer you? You have seen the life I lead, what a home with me would look like."

THE SECRET OF THE DASHING DETECTIVE

"Like your parents'?"

"Yes, something like that."

"I loved your parents' home. It was so full of love."

"Yes, but could you leave a mansion like this – one of many where you currently reside – to live in one small place?"

"Of course," she said, but Matthew heard the hitch in her tone, and he realized it was likely the first time she had actually thought this through and pictured what that life would be. Her hesitation brought him back to all of the reasons he had tried to warn them both away from this in the first place.

"Juliana," he said softly, running his hands down her arms, "just take some time and think about this. Don't rush into anything."

"When I am with you," she said, leaning into him, "Nothing else matters. I think of nothing but you. Of being with you. Of what it would feel like—"

He had to stop her there.

"Perhaps that is the problem, then," he said. "Instead, think of it when you are sitting in the middle of Warwick House, enjoying a dinner prepared by your French chef."

He said the words as gently as he could, but he knew they still stung as she started and backed away from him, immediately making him feel like an ass.

"Juliana," he said, reaching out a hand to her, but she smiled sadly at him.

"I understand," she said.

"I'm saying this to you because I care for you," he said gruffly, not used to voicing his feelings aloud, but needing her to understand. "I just want you to be sure before you go forward with anything. But know this… I care deeply for you. I do."

"I know," she said, reaching out and taking his hand in

hers, interlacing their fingers together. "And I feel the same for you. I need you to know that."

He rubbed his thumb over the back of her hand, remembering what it was like to touch her more intimately, and he nodded to the house.

"Shall we return?"

He was answered not by Juliana, however, but by a yip from the distance, and they pushed through the vegetation to find Lucy waiting for them at the fence.

"Lucy!" Juliana called out, delighted to see the dog, who seemed equally thrilled at the encounter.

She bent and petted the dog through the fence, while the mongrel tilted her head into her, accepting the affection.

Matthew watched them before coming forward himself and kneeling down next to them.

"You've gained her trust," he said quietly, extending his own hand, satisfied when the dog licked him. "Have you thought of bringing her home, of taking care of her?"

Juliana smiled ruefully. "I think of it all the time."

"Then why don't you?"

"The same reason I don't do anything I would truly like to do – because of my mother and Giles."

"What happened to going ahead and asking for forgiveness later?" he teased.

She inclined her head. "I still follow that mantra – I do. But with everything else we are going through right now, I don't want to add to their worries."

He realized, then, that as much as she had been affected by her abduction, part of the issue was that she felt guilty for what it had done to her brother, the fear it had caused within her mother.

"It wasn't your fault, Juliana."

"If I hadn't been so distracted, so easy to read—"

"It wasn't your fault," he said, more firmly now. "It was

whoever orchestrated this plan – someone I should have caught by now."

"But you are too busy looking after me."

"Not at all," he shook his head. "This is part of my job."

"Right," she said, looking back at Lucy, avoiding his gaze. "Part of your job."

"Looking after you may be the job, Juliana," he said fiercely, taking her chin in between his thumb and forefinger. "But you, Juliana – *you* are much more than a job."

If they hadn't been standing by the fence and visible to all who were passing by, he would have kissed her right then, but as it was, he would have to wait for another time, another day.

Until then, he would just have to show her how special she truly was in other ways.

CHAPTER 16

With Matthew dedicating the next few days chasing down leads consisting of her father's most vocal adversaries, Juliana did all she could to help him in his endeavors by simply staying home. It went against everything in her nature to sit and do nothing, but she passed her time helping Emma in the gardens, visiting Lucy at the fence, and working on her pamphlet, which was nearly finished.

She was quite enamoured with Matthew's drawings, and all she had to do now was find a printer who could piece it together and create the copies for her. She could hardly wait to see it on actual paper and in the hands of readers across London.

Because she didn't request his presence, she was surprised when Matthew arrived one afternoon of his own accord, a serious look on his face as he stepped into the small parlor she had occupied as her work room.

"Juliana," he greeted her once seeing that she was alone. Abigail ducked into the room after him and took a seat in the corner, so when he walked over and moved a chair to be

THE SECRET OF THE DASHING DETECTIVE

right next to her in order to speak lowly in her ear, Juliana was intrigued.

"Yes?"

"We have a bit of a... problem."

"Oh?"

"Lewis came to my office."

"Hudson Lewis? My brother?" She was so surprised that her voice rose, causing Abigail to look up from the book that Juliana had lent her. Juliana lowered her tone. "Why?"

"I had told him my name, so he asked around about me, discovered where I worked. He would like to have that dinner you mentioned."

"And?"

"I couldn't say no, and the conversation became rather awkward, so finally I had to ask him to come."

"When?"

"Friday."

"Friday! How are we to arrange your rooms by then?"

"I don't know."

Juliana stood and began muttering to herself as she paced back and forth. "We will have to make it an early dinner so that I can get away without anyone being the wiser. I shall have to go to Lady Maria and confess I have been using her as an excuse. Perhaps she will allow me to do so again, as I hardly can without asking her this time, especially for an evening event as it is hard to know where she might be, and—"

"Juliana—" He held out his hand in a halting motion. "Sit down. We will determine the best way forward. And we will do so together. Understand?"

She stopped in front of him and took a breath.

"Yes. I understand."

"Good. First, arrange a time to see Lady Maria. Then you can look at my rooms, see what you think of it, what we can do to make it better. After that we will have to arrange a menu."

He looked up at her with sudden interest. "I don't suppose you cook?"

At first her expression was one of horror, and then she couldn't help it – she began to laugh. For the thought of cooking a meal that would not only be edible but would pass as that of one a housewife would make... it was nearly too much.

Matthew seemed taken aback by her laughter at first, until finally the lines beside his eyes crinkled and he joined in. Abigail watched them as though they had gone mad, but when their chuckles finally subsided, Juliana looked at him with hands on her hips.

"We're going to have to ask for help."

* * *

HELP CAME in the form of Matthew's sister Betsy, who agreed with two stipulations – the first, that Matthew and Juliana tell her all that was transpiring, and the second, that they look after Andrew while she helped arrange the meal.

Matthew left both decisions up to Juliana, who readily agreed.

"I trust her," she explained as they stood in front of Lady Maria's building. Today was the day that Juliana would have to confess one of her sins to the woman and hope and pray that she wouldn't tell either of their mothers about what Juliana had actually been up to.

"What will you do while I speak with her?" she asked Matthew.

"I will ask the butler if I might remain in the house. It wouldn't seem right for me to be in the room with you, but I can stand sentry at the door. What do you think?"

"That is fine," she said, before reaching out and touching his arm. "Besides, I like you close."

She smiled when she noticed he had to clear his throat before following her up the stairs, Abigail trailing them. Juliana would have to speak with Abigail about their plans on Friday. Perhaps she could convince her to take a paid night off, without sharing the information with her mother or any of the other servants. It was a risk but one she might have to take.

"Lady Juliana, how wonderful to see you," Lady Maria said, as lovely as always. Juliana wondered, not for the first time, what it would have been like had Lady Maria married Giles, as was originally her mother's plan before Giles and Emma had fallen madly in love. One thing was for certain – Juliana couldn't imagine her brother and Lady Maria as anything more than partners, each serving their purpose in society. She had a difficult time picturing them as a potential love match.

Juliana thanked her and took a seat on the sofa across from her. The daughter of a wealthy marquess, Lady Maria's family home may not have been on level with Warwick House, but it was certainly luxurious in its own right.

At Lady Maria's polite but slightly inquisitive smile, Juliana decided to dispense with the pleasantries for now and get straight to the point.

"I have come to offer you an apology," Juliana said, and Lady Maria placed the cup of tea she had been pouring back on the table.

"Oh?"

"You see... I have a project about which I am quite passionate. I am actually part of a society, but it is one that my brother—" oh dear, it was awkward speaking of Giles, but she had come this far and there was no going back now, "—does not exactly approve. So I have been attending these meetings – chaperoned, of course – but I may have been telling him that I was... visiting you."

She stopped, the heat burning her cheeks, and she snuck a glance at Lady Maria to see what her response was to her confession.

To her surprise, Lady Maria was leaning forward, her elbows on her knees as she stared at Juliana in fascination.

"Do tell me more."

"More?" Juliana managed. "About..."

"Why, about your secret passion, of course. I would love to hear about whatever has you so enthralled."

"Very well," Juliana said hesitantly. "I will warn you, however, that most people do not quite understand it."

But with Lady Maria's insistence, she forged ahead, telling her of the society and their efforts. Lady Maria, raised to never interrupt, sat and listened with hands folded in her lap, the perfect audience.

Only when Juliana finished explaining did Lady Maria respond.

"Why, Lady Juliana, that is wonderful."

"Wonderful?"

"Yes, that you have so much compassion for creatures who are lesser than us. And not only that, but that you take action on it. I have much admiration for you."

"Th-thank you," Juliana said, momentarily stunned. Emma had always said she appreciated Juliana's work, but Juliana had been aware that Emma likely was just saying so because they were such good friends.

Lady Maria, however, had no reason for pretense – in fact, she had every reason to be upset with Juliana for using her as an excuse.

"You are not upset that I used you as a lie?"

"I am flattered that you would think of me," Lady Maria said with a small smile.

"But... why?"

It was now Lady Maria who seemed speechless for a moment as she paused, likely gathering her thoughts.

"Well, I suppose that I am not often thought of in that regard."

Juliana still didn't understand, and her expression must have noted that.

"I have many acquaintances, but I don't have many friends," Lady Maria finally said in a rush, and this time it was Juliana who needed time to find the right words.

"But you are so... so... *perfect*."

"According to all of our mothers, perhaps," Lady Maria said with a delicate, graceful shrug of her shoulders. "But that very same reason causes most young women – and men – to avoid me instead. And now that your brother chose another — well, I am truly happy for them both but it has caused some question as to what fault he found with me."

"I had no idea," Juliana said, suddenly feeling like a chit. She had never thought to include Lady Maria in her close circle, for her presence had always reminded her of how lesser she was than the woman she had always thought was society's darling.

"I shouldn't have said anything," Lady Maria said, dipping her head, her porcelain cheeks stained pink. "As for using me as an excuse, I do not mind. I am happy to do a small part to help."

"Thank you," Juliana said, knowing she had to ask about Friday but not knowing how to do so in any way that was genuine. "I have an... event on Friday evening that I would like to attend but—"

Lady Maria bit her lip for a moment as she thought on the dilemma.

"I am to go to a dance being held at Almack's. You could tell your mother that you are attending with me, as long as she doesn't have plans to go herself. Then she would realize that you are being untruthful, unless I can make your excuses should I see her over the night. As for how you would feign attendance without her accompaniment... that I would have to leave to you."

"You would do that for me?"

"I would be happy to."

"I don't know how to thank you."

"Continue to do your work," Lady Maria said, which only caused Juliana further shame when in fact she was going to be with Matthew on Friday night.

"Perhaps you could call upon me next week?" Juliana asked, surprised to realize that she earnestly meant the invitation – she did want to see Lady Maria again, was interested in spending time in her company.

"I would like that very much," replied Lady Maria, obviously trying to quickly hide her pleasure. "Thank you."

They spent the remainder of the visit engaged in deeper conversation than they had ever partaken in before, despite the fact they had spent a rather good amount of time together – although most of it was with their mothers, which meant that it was hard to get a word in, and if they did, it was often led in the direction of conversation their mothers preferred.

When it was time to depart, Juliana said her farewell with much warmth, and was practically brimming with excitement when she and Matthew left.

"Next stop? Holborn," Matthew said with a grim smile. "We will collect Betsy and then continue on to my boarding house."

Juliana clasped her hands together in excitement as they boarded the carriage, eager to see what his living quarters looked like. They picked up Betsy and Andrew on the way, and when they arrived in front of a two-storey brown building, Juliana gazed out of the window in curiosity. Abigail agreed to stay in the carriage with James atop it – Betsy assured her that she would be a proper chaperone – and they followed Matthew into his building.

Juliana wasn't sure what she expected of Matthew's living quarters. But when she stepped through the door she was quite... underwhelmed.

The apartment was neat and tidy, which she appreciated. But besides that, it was sparse, plain. Why, if she hadn't known better, she would have wondered whether anyone lived here.

She turned to ask him why he had no adornments anywhere, but Betsy obviously guessed at what she was thinking.

"Matthew has always said he was too busy to make this a true home," she said with pursed lips as she put Andrew down and allowed him to explore this new place. "I think he just always knew there was something else waiting for him."

She placed a knowing look upon first Juliana and then Matthew before continuing into the room, arms crossed over her chest. She looked back at Juliana.

"Now, my lady, what do you think we should do to make this place a home?"

CHAPTER 17

Matthew's head was spinning by the time Juliana and Betsy were finished. They sat together, planning and scheming, deciding Betsy and Mary would set everything in motion before Friday. Juliana would have liked to have taken part in much of it herself, but it would be too difficult for her to find enough excuses to get away.

Matthew had enjoyed watching her play with Andrew more than he would have liked to admit. It wasn't hard to picture Juliana as a mother someday, although he had to remind himself more than once that it wouldn't be to his children, and that the nobility mothered in a much different manner than he was familiar.

He had returned to his office now to convene with his men and see if any of them had made any strides forward in following down the leads he had assigned to them all.

"Anderson?" he started, but the man was already shaking his head.

"The lord he won all of the money off is dead. Couldn't

have been him. He had no living relatives who would take issue, either."

"Pip?" he asked after nodding his thanks to Anderson.

"The banker he caused to lose his job received it back and doesn't seem to hold any ill will. That being said, I still followed up. He wasn't in London at the time of the duke's death."

Matthew continued around the room, but each lead died, one after another.

"Green?" he finished, hoping that he could count on Owen to have some good news for him.

"I've continued to follow up with Lewis, but he doesn't seem to have any interaction with the family. The night of Lady Juliana's abduction, he was at his mother's house, as far as we can tell."

Matthew nodded. "That's good, although I don't suppose his mother is necessarily a trustworthy source, either."

"They could certainly be in this together."

"Very well," Matthew said with some resignation. His own assignment for the week had been to ascertain Lord Hemingway's movements during the time in question, but from what he can tell, the man had been out of the city, in Bath. "So, we have made no progress."

"We have made *some* progress," Owen corrected him, and Matthew looked up, trying not to hold onto too much hope.

"How so?"

"We further questioned Cillian Reynolds, like you asked."

"The man who admitted to abducting Lady Juliana."

He had kept his usual composure when he had met with the man before, but that was before... before he had begun to feel anything for Juliana.

Now, if he came face to face with him, knowing that the man had placed his hands on her to carry her away and cause such fear within her, he likely wouldn't be able to keep himself from doing something he would never be able to come back from.

"Did he have anything new to say?"

"Actually, he did," Owen said with a self-satisfied smile. "He told us more about who hired him."

"Did he, now?"

"He said he received the instructions on a note – one that he gave us."

"Let me see." Matthew held out his hand.

Owen passed over the piece of paper. It was crinkled, dirty now, after being in Reynolds' possession for so long, but that couldn't hide the fact that the paper was of some quality, and the ink and hand upon it had been written by someone of breeding.

"It was someone from the nobility, then," Matthew said grimly. "Or, at least, a profession."

He had suspected it, based on the fact that whoever they were after seemed to know the family's movements, had understood the ways of society. But it would also make it much more difficult to persecute someone of high status – even if their victim had been a duke.

"Well, at least we can narrow our search," he said, tapping his fingers on the desk. "Let's look at the duke's enemies again, but this time narrow it to those who would be in society. We should also consider servants of the household who might have aided the perpetrator. People who would know where the duke would be, what he would eat, when he would eat. Remember, the original duke was poisoned, and whoever captured Lady Juliana knew where she would be and what would distract her. And..." the thought, the one that had been niggling at him for some time now finally bloomed. "Someone who would have known the duke well enough to be aware that he does not sleep in the duke's chambers. When someone went after him while they were in the country, it was in the room he was sleeping in."

"Very good, Archibald," Owen said, before they moved on to next steps and other issues of the day.

Matthew tried to concentrate – this was his business, after all, and he should know all of the details of what was happening – but he was having difficulty focusing on anything but Juliana and their dinner tomorrow night. Dinner with Hudson Lewis, a man who, through no fault of his own, was becoming less of a suspect, and more of a friend.

* * *

So far, everything had miraculously gone to plan.

Juliana had convinced her mother that she was accompanying Lady Maria to Lady Merryweather's ball at Almack's. Her mother, of course, had immediately suggested that she and Juliana attend the event along with Lady Maria and her mother, Lady Bennington, but then Prudence had helpfully reminded their mother that they were to attend a musicale Friday evening. Juliana's presence could be excused, but it would be the height of rudeness if all three chose to attend another event after confirming their attendance.

Their mother bit her lip, obviously trying to determine how to make her excuses for the musicale. She told Prudence that they would make an appearance at the musicale before leaving for Almack's, prompting Juliana to write Lady Maria a note regarding her mother's plans. Hopefully, if Lady Maria encountered her, she would be able to make excuses for her, and by the time Juliana's mother returned, Juliana would be well in bed.

She had then bribed Abigail into taking the night off after leaving with her. Fortunately, she had a beau she was eager to visit, and she agreed to the paid night off along with additional payment from Juliana as well as a promise that should her mother ever find out, Juliana would ensure that Abigail found an excellent placement elsewhere.

Matthew had arrived at Warwick House for Juliana, and walked both her and Abigail down the street to a hack. They rode with Abigail as far as her mother's house where she bid them farewell, before Matthew and Juliana began to make their way to Matthew's home.

Juliana tapped her fingers against her knees, suddenly nervous at being alone with Matthew, especially as they would be posing as husband and wife and acting for Lewis – her brother.

Matthew seemed to understand her fears as he leaned in and placed his hands on top of hers to still her nervous tapping.

"Do not worry."

"Do not worry?" she said, raising her eyebrows. "How can you say that? There is everything to be worried about!"

"Betsy has everything prepared. The apartments look well lived in. You already know how to be the perfect hostess."

She turned her hands over so that her palms were against his and squeezed his hands.

"Thank you."

"Of course," he said before turning to look out the window, and Juliana was caught by the way the light struck his cheekbones. She wanted nothing more than to wrap her arms around him and revel in his warmth, in all of the comfort he could give her, but she didn't want him to know how close to the edge she was. So instead, she stayed in her seat, her hands in his, and waited for the hack to stop.

* * *

"Here we are," Matthew said, leading Juliana inside. "Home sweet home."

He watched her jaw drop open as she looked around her, and he couldn't help his grin.

"Not the same place you remember?" he asked.

"No, not at all. It is… well, it is… perfect!"

"Betsy and Mary put your vision into actuality, that is certain," he said. "Let me show you where everything is in the kitchen."

He led her in, showing her the dishes Betsy and Mary had prepared, with instructions on what she needed to do in order to finish them.

"How wonderful that they have made so many dishes of vegetables," she said, touched that Matthew's sisters would think of such a thing.

"They made one meat dish in order to ensure it would suffice for Lewis, but the rest they made to your preference," he said. "In addition, it should be easy enough to make the last preparations."

"I should have asked Abigail to come," she murmured. "It would make sense for us to have a maid, wouldn't it?"

"Perhaps yes, perhaps no," he said. "But it would have been another opportunity for Lewis to ascertain the truth."

"That makes sense," she said as she continued to look around her in both interest and astonishment. "When will he arrive?" she asked.

"Any moment now," Matthew said, and at her agitation, he knew he needed to calm her. He stood in front of her and looped his arms around her hips, pulling her close.

"All will be fine," he said.

"You do not know that," she said, shaking her head.

"Perhaps I don't, that is true," he admitted. "But I know that no matter what happens, I will be here for you and you for me. That is enough, is it not?"

"I suppose it shall have to be," she said with a small smile, and Matthew couldn't help but lean in and kiss her on the nose.

A noise sounded from outside the door – a shuffle more than anything, and Matthew broke away from Juliana right before the knock sounded. She stayed a step behind him as he walked to the door, opening it with the smile on his face – until he saw just who was on the other side, standing next to Lewis.

"Mr. Archibald, it is good to see you," Lewis said with a smile. "Thank you again for having me. I hope it is no inconvenience, but to even out numbers and make all more comfortable for your wife, I brought a guest. May I introduce my mother?"

CHAPTER 18

His mother? Juliana brought a hand to her mouth. It was one thing to get to know her half-brother, but the woman with whom her father had been unfaithful to her mother? Well, that was something else entirely. She straightened her spine as she pasted a smile on her face, reminding herself of why they were doing this – to find justice for whomever was coming after her family – but it wasn't enough to prepare her for what was to come next.

The pair had stepped into the room, but no one had yet said anything besides Dr. Lewis. That was odd, wasn't it? Surely Matthew and Mrs. Lewis should have made their pleasantries by now.

"I know you." Mrs. Lewis' voice was low, perhaps usually holding a pleasant tone, but with that statement, it held a hint of menace in it.

"I am from the neighbourhood," Matthew said, friendliness still held in his words. "I'm sure we must have seen one another a time or two."

"No, that is not it. I *know* you. I have spoken to you before."

Oh, dear. This couldn't be good.

"Perhaps my work has allowed us to meet?" he said, obviously attempting to keep things light.

"You came to my door," she said, a finger raised before her, pointed at his chest. "You and that—that—man."

Juliana wrung her hands together. She had thought of many ways this could have gone wrong, but she had never considered that it would have gone *this* wrong. She wasn't sure who *that man* was, but she couldn't help but wonder whether it was Giles.

"Ah, yes, we did have the fortune to meet," Matthew said. "Perhaps now we can actually get to know one another better."

The woman stepped fully into the room now, closer to Matthew, giving Juliana her first chance to properly see her. She was tall, and of similar age to Juliana's mother. An air of beauty still surrounded her, although her hair now included streaks of grey and there were many more wrinkles around her eyes than there would have been when Juliana's father had known her.

"You came with *him* – the man raised by that monster. To question me about whether I had taken that girl. When in truth, I want nothing to do with any of that family. I never did."

Juliana supposed she could understand the woman's sentiment, but the statement still hurt, nonetheless.

"Mother," Dr. Lewis said in a measured tone, "I am not sure what you are speaking about, but why don't we sit down and discuss this further?"

"This man," she said, pointing to Matthew once more, "works for the son of the man who sired you."

Juliana's heart jumped as she saw Dr. Lewis look from Matthew to his mother and back again.

"If that is the case, I am sure it must be a coincidence,"

he said. "I met Mr. Archibald and his wife by chance. Let me introduce you to *Mrs.* Archibald and then we can all sit—"

Mrs. Lewis' gaze finally swung to Juliana, recognition entering her eyes. Juliana didn't think she had ever seen the woman before, although she did have an aspect of familiarity.

"Mrs. Archibald? Ha. Another lie."

"Mrs. Lewis," Juliana said, stepping forward with a hand outstretched. "Perhaps we should—"

"This, son," Mrs. Lewis continued with that finger out again, "is none other than Lady Juliana Remington, who is the sister of the Duke of Warwick – also sired by *that man*. And unless a miracle has transpired – which I am highly in doubt of – she is *not* married to this investigator."

Dr. Lewis stopped, frozen now, as he stared at Juliana before looking back at his mother.

Finally, he spoke, although it seemed he wasn't entirely sure what to say.

"It is hard to know where to begin," he said in slow, measured tones and a calmness that would be required in his profession, "with the fact that my father was a duke, that I have half-siblings, or that the two of you have been lying to me for reasons unknown."

"None of it matters," his mother said, wrapping her arm around his elbow. "We are going."

"Please don't," Juliana said, surprising them all by stepping forward. "There is so much I would like to speak to you about."

"Their family is poisonous," Mrs. Lewis said, her eyes narrowing, and Juliana reminded herself that it was not her fault the woman held such sentiments, but her father's – like so many things in her life had been. "We must go."

Dr. Lewis stared at them for a moment as though uncertain what to say but seemed resigned to follow his mother out.

Just before he turned from them, after his mother had already started down the hall, Juliana silently touched his arm, and when he looked back, she placed her card in his hand. He said nothing, made no reaction, but he did pocket it – leaving Juliana with some hope.

* * *

"Well," Matthew said, collapsing into a chair. "That was... unexpected."

Juliana paced back and forth in front of him, across the carpet that Matthew's sisters had added at her suggestion. At first she had been reluctant to make the recommendations, unsure of who would pay for it all, but Matthew had assured her that he could afford it – it had more been a matter of time and taste than whether he had the money.

"Did you have any idea he would bring his mother?"

"None," he said, not enjoying seeing her agitation, even though he had a similar sensation deep in his own chest.

"He is never going to forgive us. Never. Just when I thought that perhaps we could build a relationship with him, that I could get to know him better, that I had gained another brother—"

"Juliana," he said, knowing he needed to stop her before she became too upset to think clearly. "There was never any way that we were going to be able to honestly befriend Lewis unless he knew our true identities. Otherwise, it was all based on a lie, one that he was bound to discover, especially when you never had a child."

"I know," she said, flinging her hands up in the air. "I know you're right. I simply feel... wretched. I never should have thought this would work. I never should have done any of this. I just..." she stopped and stared at him. "I suppose I just liked the thought of getting to know him better. And I especially liked the thought of being your wife."

He stood from the large, overstuffed armchair he occupied whenever he took a moment to actually relax in his quarters and began walking over to her, stopping when he was right in front of her. He looked down at her hands, taking them in his.

"I shouldn't admit this," he surprised himself by saying. "Not to you or to myself. But I liked it too."

She looked up, her lips but a breath away from his.

"Has it all fallen apart?"

He reached up and tucked an errant lock of hair behind her ear.

"Some of it has, that is for certain," he murmured. "But not all of it. Certainly not all of it."

She had initiated so many of their kisses, but this time it was different. This time it was his lips coming to hers, claiming them, reminding her that no matter what society said, no matter what the wise decision would be when their future together was near impossible, he would leave her with kisses so great and memorable that no one else would ever compare.

He should be ashamed of doing so, but he couldn't be. Not when it came to Juliana. For if this was the way he would claim her, by making love to her lips, then claim her he would.

"Matthew," she murmured against his mouth when they paused to take a breath, her fingers inching up his chest until they made their way to loop around his shoulders and she pulled him in closer to her. "You make me feel... everything."

He bent his head into her shoulder and inhaled the sweetness of her scent, like gingerbread at Christmas.

"I know, Jules," he said. "I know."

"Make me feel more," she said, looking up at him with glistening eyes, but he was already shaking his head.

"I cannot," he said, even as his hands slid up and down her back, drawing her in closer.

"Why not?" she whispered.

"Because you are for someone else. Not for me, an investigator who could never give you the life that you deserve."

She gripped his cheeks between her hands and stared up into his eyes.

"Do you not understand? I. Do. Not. Care. You are Matthew and that is all that matters to me. *You* are the man that I am falling in love with."

Her words both took him higher than he had ever been before in his life and also brought him to his knees as he tried to imagine himself as ever worthy of her. He was not a man who had issues in seeing himself in a good light, but she was also Lady Juliana Remington, sister of a duke. He was a detective. It would be a scandal of the highest level if she were to ever sully herself with him.

"I—" He wanted to tell her he loved her, yet he knew that would only further her resolve to be with him, here and now, and he could not have that. He needed her to have some hesitation, for he wasn't sure that he held enough for the both of them. "I can bring you pleasure. That I can do."

Her smile widened, her lips stretching wide on her face, and he resolved that he would make her happier than she had ever been before – even if it was just for this one night. He bent and scooped her up in his arms, to which she gave a small "oomph!" of surprise before he carried her through the room and into his bedroom down the hall. He hadn't shown her the room when she had visited the other day, and his sisters hadn't done anything to make it comfortable like the rest of the home. It was still the neat but sparse bed in the neat but sparse room with nary anything on the walls.

But she didn't seem to care, so at the moment, neither did he.

He placed her reverently down upon the bed, shucking his jacket before he leaned over her, but he didn't touch her – instead he reached behind her and began to loosen her hair, pulling out one pin after the other. He had yearned to see her with her hair spread out around her, the thought of it, especially upon his bedsheets, erotic. He continued with her watching him until he was finished and her hair waved around the front and back of her shoulders. As he gazed down on her, he knew that this image of her would forever hold a space in his mind – the soft cream of her dress upon his dark blue blankets, her cheeks rosy and her green eyes filled with desire – for him.

If only he could have her. If it wasn't for the great differences spread between them, he was ready to give her all of him and to take whatever she had to offer in return. The only problem was that she was *too* giving, and he knew she would likely give more than she should.

He crawled over the bed toward her, stopping when he reached her waist. He knelt overtop of her, tugging the bottom of her bodice down, one inch at a time, until her perfect, creamy, pert breasts were bared to him. He took first one and then the other into his mouth as she gasped above him and dug her fingers into his shoulders.

He lightly scraped his teeth over her nipples as his hands began to explore her body through the confines of her dress. Finally, he had enough, and he reached behind her and began to undo the buttons, pausing halfway down.

"I am so sorry – do you mind? Say the word and I will stop, I promise—"

"Do. Not. Stop."

She was forceful when she wanted something – that was for certain.

And he liked it.

He tugged her dress off her body but left her chemise where it was, although it didn't leave much to his imagination. At least it was one last barrier between them, to keep him from going further to discover what was underneath.

He ran his hand up one smooth calf, over her thigh, until he reached the center between her legs, finding the nub of pleasure, which he began to stroke as he returned his tongue to one of her nipples.

"Matthew," she gasped again. "Oh, Matthew, this is... this is..."

She didn't have to describe it, however, for he could see the words written on her face. She had been amused before, yes, but now she was enthralled. And he was the one making her feel this way.

"Can I continue?" he asked, and she nodded.

"Please," she said with a moan, and he slipped a finger inside of her, causing her entire body to tremble.

He kept going, in and out, as his own thoughts became hazy, his desire matching hers while his mouth travelled over her body, kissing her through the bunched fabric of her chemise as he went lower and lower still.

He had never wanted a woman with such intensity, and he was having a difficult time remembering that there would be no finish for him, that this was about her, and so he branded her with everything he could give her.

His mouth reached the bottom of her chemise, and he moved his hand to make room for his tongue.

"Matthew, what are you—oh!" she exclaimed as he found her, seemingly barely able to contain herself as he held her against him and tasted the very essence of her. He looked up so that he could continue to enjoy her while seeing what she looked like – and she looked like the goddess that she was, her cheeks flushed, her back arching into the air. His hands wrapped around her buttocks, holding her close even as she writhed against him, looking for more though likely uncertain of just what that more was. His tongue continued to move, tasting, exploring, and she was trembling around him again.

"Come for me," he said, even though he wasn't entirely sure that she knew exactly what he meant by that.

"I—I just—what you are doing, it's too good, it's—it's *sorcery.*"

He couldn't help but laugh at that, which must have felt good against her for she reached down and gripped his hair as he returned to the center of all her feeling and moved hard and fast. She cried out, and he hoped that his neighbours couldn't hear her through the walls.

When she finally went lax against him, he stared up at her, unable to stop the words that poured from his lips.

"You are the most beautiful woman I've ever seen," he said. "And you are mine."

He saw the flash of triumph in her eyes, and he had to add, for the benefit of them both, "for now."

"You are right," she said, lifting him up to her, whipping off his cravat and fisting his shirt in her hands. "I am yours. And I want you to make me yours. In truth, every way possible."

CHAPTER 19

"We cannot."

She knew what he was going to say before the words were even out of his mouth, and she was already doing her utmost to change his mind.

"We can."

"Juliana—"

"Matthew, you were right when you said that I am yours. And you are mine. Whatever happens in the future will happen, but one thing I know for certain is that I will never feel for another the way I feel for you. No one else will ever do for me what you just did, and I know that no one will ever love as you will."

"Your brother would murder me."

"Do we really need to speak about my brother at a time like this?"

He couldn't help but chuckle at that as he stared at her, shaking his head.

"Do you know how orderly my life was before I met you?"

"I think I have an idea."

THE SECRET OF THE DASHING DETECTIVE

She stood on her knees then and lifted the chemise over her head, depositing it on the floor beside her. When she saw his eyes roam over her, the obvious swallow of his throat, she knew that she had him.

She leaned over him, taking his lips, and knowing that he wanted this as much as she did. She pulled him back with her on the bed, wrapping her legs around his waist as she reached down and began to search for the fall of his breeches, even though she had no idea what to do to release him.

He was now with her, however, as he made quick work of them, soon down to his linen shirt between them. She lifted it up and with one strong arm he was rid of it, until they were bare, skin on skin, and it was the most glorious thing she had ever felt in her life.

She wasn't sure what to do here, either, but one thing she knew – his prominent erection jutting toward her was what she needed to make them one, to allow her to feel everything she had been waiting for. She reached out and ran her fingers lightly over it and when he groaned, she figured she was doing something right.

As he kissed her again, he reached his hand down and flicked at the bud of pleasure she'd had no idea existed until a few minutes ago, and she knew what he was doing – getting her ready to go to that place again, the one where she felt every bit of elation that was possible in a matter of seconds. Would she get there again? She had no idea, but she would do anything to make it so.

"Please," she muttered, and he leaned in and nipped at her neck.

"Are you asking for something?"

She reached out and slapped him lightly, which surprised him enough that he paused the kiss for a second and she felt his smile against her lips.

"Are you sure?"

"Never more."

He lowered himself to her entrance and began sliding into her.

Juliana wasn't sure what to prepare for, but he murmured, "relax, love," in her ear, and she tried to do so as he went slowly, filling her inch by inch. She wasn't sure it was possible that they would fit together, but she felt the moment her body seemed to accept him, when it actually did relax enough for the two of them to meld together as one. There had been a moment of sharp pain, but it passed quickly enough as he stilled within her, obviously giving her time to get used to what was happening.

She didn't need long.

"More," she said, and he responded by slowly sliding out, and then back in.

"Does that feel all right?"

"Yes," she said, and he did the same thing again, until she became impatient, wondering if they could go any faster – and decided that there was only one thing to do, which was to take control of the speed herself.

She lifted her hips up to meet him, and he seemed to understand what she needed as he began rocking into her faster, and while she had felt the pleasure before, now it was another sensation entirely. Then he changed the angle of his thrust so that he was rubbing against her, even as he kissed her with such tenderness that she knew what he felt for her, even if he wouldn't say it out loud.

The sensations began building within her again, until she was trembling around him, and her entire world exploded in a kaleidoscope of color. She was just coming down from it when he pulled out of her abruptly and she opened her eyes in time to seem him wiping himself off beside her.

Then he was back above her, and he kissed her on the

forehead, the nose, the cheek, the jaw, as they stared at one another in complete and utter amazement.

He opened his mouth, but she took her index finger to his chin and closed it before he could say anything.

"Don't say it."

"I—"

"Don't. That was wonderful and amazing and everything I could ever ask for. That I *did* ask for. Whatever happens, I will remember that for the rest of my life."

"As will I," he finally said, the smile she was waiting for finally crossing his face. "As will I. Now, as much as I would like to keep you here in my bed all evening, I think we've had enough excitement for one night. I wouldn't want to stretch our luck."

He stood, pulling on his clothing before helping her to her feet. "Come, let's get you fed. Then it's time for me to take you home."

* * *

MATTHEW FELT like he was walking on the sun the next day after his night with Juliana. There was the part of him that kept reminding him that he had made a colossal mistake, of course, but he tried to silence that aspect of his mind, and instead, for one day at least, focus on Juliana and all they had shared together.

He was a fool to care for her, he knew that, but care for her he did – he might even go further than that to say he loved her, although he was not quite ready to admit that to himself.

By the time he entered his office, he was humming to himself, but stopped when he entered the door and found a few of his men staring at him.

"Archibald?"

"Yes, Owen?"

"You have a visitor."

His head snapped up and he looked to the side of the room where the few guest chairs sat, shocked to find Hudson Lewis standing in front of them, waiting for him.

"Lewis," he said calmly, "come with me into my office."

He shut the door behind the two of them, gesturing to the chair in front of his desk. Matthew decided to get right to the point of the matter.

"I will not insult you by offering my apologies. I can, however, provide an explanation if that is what you are after."

Lewis sat calmly and folded his hands over each other in his lap.

"I would appreciate that. It doesn't take much to shock me, but I was quite taken aback by all that I learned last night, that is for certain. Unfortunately, my mother was not extremely forthcoming about my father and my background. She never has been, and nothing changed when part of the truth emerged yesterday. I was hoping you could fill in some of the gaps."

"Very well," Matthew said, leaning back in his chair as he drummed his fingertips on the desk in front of him, trying to determine how much to share with Lewis. Finally, he decided that he had nothing to lose by telling him everything he knew about the man's own background and family history and went ahead and did so. He told him about how they discovered his connection to the duke's family through the ledgers, what happened to the duke, and even that they had considered Lewis a potential suspect. He told him that Juliana was never supposed to be a part of it, but she had insisted upon taking part in the scheme because of how much she wanted to meet the half-brother she never knew she had.

"I'm not sure if it means anything, but she never believed that you were guilty," he said. "She enjoyed the opportunity to get to know you and was greatly aggrieved last night after you left."

"I see," Lewis said, steepling his fingers together. "It was quite an unfortunate evening. I cannot say that I enjoy being lied to, although I cannot help but be somewhat interested in learning more about the family."

"There is one thing that I can tell you," Matthew said. "From what I have learned, the children are not at all like the man I am told the duke was. I never met him personally, but by all accounts, he was not a good man. I have, however, enjoyed working with the current duke."

"And the ladies Juliana and Prudence?" Lewis said with a slight, knowing look.

"They are fine people as well," Matthew finished rather blandly. "The dowager duchess might require some time to get used to the idea of all of you knowing one another."

"I see," Lewis said, before standing. "Well, if they would like to know more about me, then I suppose there is no time like the present."

"The present?"

"Yes," Lewis said. "Do you mind showing me where they live?"

* * *

JULIANA WAS both surprised and pleased when Lady Maria called upon her the day after she had been with Matthew.

"How lovely to see you!" she said, before nodding at Lady Bennington, who followed in behind her. Of course, Lady Maria would always travel properly chaperoned – although, so too did most young women of the *ton*. Juliana chastised herself, reminding herself that she *liked* Lady Maria, and she should no longer be thinking any ill of her.

"It is good to see you are recovered, Lady Juliana," Lady Bennington said.

Juliana murmured a brief "of course," before catching Lady Maria's gaze.

As Juliana's mother, Emma, and Prudence welcomed Lady Bennington, Juliana drew Lady Maria to the side of the room.

"Was everything well last night?" she asked her softly.

"Yes, for the most part," Lady Maria whispered back. "Your mother did appear and asked after you, but I told her you had left with a headache. My mother seemed most interested in where you had been, but I quickly distracted her. We just must make sure that they do not speak in detail on the subject, or it will be difficult to maintain the lie. My mother was insistent on accompanying me to visit today."

"That is just fine," Juliana said, although her heartbeat had kicked up a notch. "Thank you so much for your assistance in all of this."

"Of course," Lady Maria said with a wide, pretty smile. "I am happy to help."

They took a seat on one side of the drawing room near Prudence and Emma, while Lady Bennington and the dowager duchess were on the other side, near the tea service.

"Now, do tell me about last night," Lady Maria said quietly in her ear, her eyes shining, and Lady Juliana tried to think of a plausible explanation besides that last night had been the greatest experience of her life, but just then the butler, Jameson, entered the room.

"Your Grace," he said, to Lady Emma, "you have another visitor."

He crossed the room and passed her a card.

Lady Emma's eyes widened, and she looked up, meeting

Juliana's eyes before flicking them to Juliana's mother with some hesitancy.

All in the room were now staring at her, and she stood, walking to the door. "If you shall excuse me for one moment," she said, as Jameson followed her out.

After a short, awkward silence, conversation resumed, although it was quickly overwhelmed by activity in the hall.

"Your Grace, the drawing room is already occupied, perhaps you might want to enter the parlor—"

"Is Lady Juliana here?" Oh dear. The 'Your Grace' in question was Giles. This couldn't be good.

"She is in the drawing room as well. Your Grace, you have visitors—"

But Giles, apparently, didn't overly care. He was the duke, yes, but he also did not contain as much regard for social niceties as he should have.

"Juliana?" he said, standing in the door, Emma behind him, tugging on his elbow.

"Yes?"

"I believe you have some explaining to do."

And there, caught in the light of the hall, was a man Juliana recognized all too well.

Her other brother.

CHAPTER 20

Matthew had a feeling that this exchange was not going to end well – not when the dowager duchess was in the house and especially not when she had company.

Upon his arrival with Lewis, Jameson had left them waiting in the foyer while he sought out the duchess. In the meantime, the duke had arrived home and demanded an explanation for how Lewis knew about their family, which Matthew had offered as best he could, although he wished he could have done so without Lewis present, for now he was basically admitting his sins twice before the man. He omitted Juliana's role in his explanation, but Lewis had made it clear that he had already met her, prompting the expected questions from the duke.

Which led to their current situation.

They all sat in the drawing room now, after Lady Bennington and her daughter had made a hasty departure, although not before Lady Maria and Lewis had exchanged a good deal of interested glances at one another. Matthew wasn't sure what that was about – had they met before? – but he soon put the thought behind him as there was so much else to concern himself with.

Such as the fact the dowager duchess was present for Lewis' introduction.

"Well," Matthew said when it seemed that no one else was going to say anything. He was also trying his utmost not to stare at Juliana, sitting across from him with wide eyes and pink lips that he was now far too well acquainted with. "I would like to introduce Hudson Lewis, of whom you all know. Dr. Lewis, this is the Duke and Duchess of Warwick, the dowager duchess of Warwick, Lady Juliana, and Lady Prudence. Ah, and here is Lady Winchester now."

Lewis nodded at them each in turn before sitting forward with his hands folded in front of him, elbows on knees.

"This is a rather awkward situation, of that I am aware," he said. "I wasn't certain how to handle it myself, but I just discovered my background last night and was… interested to learn more."

"What do you want from us?" the dowager duchess said rather sharply.

Lady Juliana countered with, "Mother!"

Lewis was not fazed.

"I want nothing. I have a successful practice as a physician, and I have no need for anything further. I simply wanted to meet those who I have just learned are my half-siblings. I am also here to tell you that I had nothing to do with the death of the previous duke. In fact, I did not even know that he was my father until yesterday."

The dowager duchess sniffed but said nothing more.

"We are glad you came," Juliana said with some hesitation. "I know when I met you that I was not truthful, and for that I apologize. If it is of any consolation, I never thought that you had anything to do with my father's death."

"And where, Juliana, did you have chance to meet with

Dr. Lewis?" her mother asked sharply, and Juliana's cheeks colored.

"I was out one day, and we happened to encounter him. Mr. Archibald was already befriending him, and he just happened to be accompanying me on an errand when we ran across Dr. Lewis."

"I see," the dowager duchess said. It was clear she had further questions but had no wish to ask them now with Lewis in the room.

"Perhaps I should not have come," Lewis said. "But I will provide my address if you have any wish to speak further."

He rose to leave, but it was the duke who stepped forward now, between Lewis and the entrance.

"That will not be necessary," he said. "We are glad you sought us out. Please, have a seat. You must stay for dinner."

"You do not have to—"

"I insist," the duke said, and Matthew could see the similarities in features between the two half-brothers. The duke walked over to Matthew and held out his hand. "Thank you, Archibald," he said. "I believe we can close the door on this subject. We shall see you tomorrow."

Matthew took his hand even as he realized that he was, effectively, being dismissed. He nodded at the duke, turning for one last glance at Juliana before he left. She was staring at him, the look on her face telling him to stay, but for what reason?

Lewis was welcomed, for he was part of their family now. Matthew? He was nothing. Nothing but the hired help.

* * *

IT WAS interesting how one's life could change so drastically in such a short time.

Most of Juliana's life had been rather dull, with the exception of her work with her animal welfare society. But everything else was a monotonous routine of doing what was expected of her, with the only changes being small pieces of gossip that meant nothing in the grand scheme of the world. Even her father's death had only served to provide her greater freedom.

But now everything had changed. She had a half-brother, one who most of her family – with the exception of her mother – seemed to accept. She had made love to a man, and not just any man, but a man who had also captured her heart. If only she knew what a life together would look like, it would make future discussions easier. One thing she did know, however, was that she wasn't ready to give up the opportunity to be with him.

Before moving forward with Matthew, however, she had to speak with another man. One who likely had also seen the future much differently than it was going to turn out, for both of them.

Lord Hemingway had asked to call upon her this afternoon, and she had agreed – but only because she knew she had to tell him the truth. That she did not love him, and she could not marry him.

She was sure the first would be no surprise – at no point had either of them declared any feelings for one another, and nor were any expected. But she had an inkling that Lord Hemingway and both of their mothers had been fairly certain that the latter was a given, when, in fact, she knew now that everything she had assumed to be true – that all she needed in life was a man to provide financial and moral support – was utterly wrong.

She hoped he would take it well, that he would be amenable to finding another to take her place.

She just wasn't sure how her mother would react.

Juliana looked up at her now from her place on the settee

in the drawing room. She would have preferred to be putting the finishing touches on the pamphlet that would be going to print tomorrow, but she could never risk her mother seeing the publication. Instead, she was mutilating the needlework in front of her. She had started the work attempting a sun and cloud but it was currently looking more like potatoes and gravy.

"How lovely that Lord Hemingway is taking you for a ride today," her mother said, beaming at her.

"Yes," Juliana said, knowing better than to tell her mother her true purpose, for her mother would only try to dissuade her.

"He is such a gentleman," her mother continued. "And from such a good family."

"He is from our family," Juliana said wryly, and her mother tsked at her.

"That is not what I mean," she said. "His father was your father's cousin. That is not so very close. And his mother is the most wonderful woman I have met."

"It *is* lovely that the two of you were able to remain such good friends over the years," Juliana said truthfully, leaving out the last bit – that it was lovely, despite that their husbands, who were relatives, were neither faithful nor kind to their wives.

"How marvelous it will be to have the family truly together," her mother continued dreamily.

Juliana had to stifle her words, grateful when the knock sounded on the door and Jameson stood within the entrance.

"Lord Hemingway has arrived," he said, to which the dowager duchess nodded.

"Thank you, Jameson," she said before turning to Juliana. "It is probably best you are leaving the house, for we would not want a repeat of yesterday with Lord Hemingway here. It was embarrassment enough that Lady Bennington and Lady

Maria had to see such a spectacle. Well, off you go. You do look lovely today, Juliana. Be sure to take your white bonnet with the yellow ribbon. Is Abigail prepared?"

"Yes, she is ready with the bonnet," Juliana said, leaning in and surprising her mother by placing a kiss on her cheek. She knew what she was about to do would upset her mother, and while it was necessary, she did feel sorry for distressing her. "I shall see you soon."

Juliana started down the front stairs on Lord Hemingway's arm, somewhat jolted in surprise when she saw Matthew waiting on his horse to the side of the drive. He said nothing, instead simply nodding at her, and she swallowed. Of course he was here. Giles would have been sure that he was nearby for a ride in the park. It seemed that Giles didn't think much of Lord Hemingway's ability to protect her, either.

Lord Hemingway helped her up into his phaeton and she sat on the seat, knowing that going out with him would cause the gossips to assume that their union was all but settled. She didn't know where else to tell him of what she was feeling, however, for otherwise their mothers would be present and that would be the ultimate disaster.

The phaeton set into motion with Matthew trotting behind them on his horse, and Juliana had an inexplicable urge to jump out of the carriage and climb up behind him and ride away with him.

Which, of course, she would never do. But she couldn't help considering it.

Juliana had to time this just right. She allowed Lord Hemingway to speak about everything and nothing as they left Piccadilly and entered the park. There, they made pleasantries and waved to people they knew as all watched them with interest.

Lord Hemingway eventually pulled the phaeton over to

the side of the path near the bank of the Serpentine and Juliana had a feeling something was coming – something she needed to stop before it went too far.

"Lady Juliana," Lord Hemingway said, clearing his throat as though he had something important to say. "I have quite enjoyed the time we have spent together."

"As have I," Juliana said as quickly as she could, before he was able to say anymore. "I am most grateful for the attention you have paid me, and you must know that you are a very kind man, who will make a wonderful husband one day."

"I am glad you think so," he said before she could continue. "For—

"But not to me," Juliana said in a rush. "I know that this is the height of rudeness, I do, and I am so sorry, Lord Hemingway, but I cannot marry you."

He looked at her blankly, the only sign he was still alive the few times he blinked. Finally, he managed, "I thought we were courting."

"We were," she said, placing her gloved hand on his, wishing she could make this right but uncertain how exactly to do so. "I wish things were different, but I have come to realize that I need to marry for love, and I think we are both aware that while we get on well, we simply do not have that love for one another."

"It will grow... through marriage," he insisted, but Juliana was shaking her head.

"I am very sorry, Lord Hemingway," she said. "Perhaps we should return now."

He was stone-faced as he turned from her and called tersely to his driver to take them back to Warwick House. Juliana looked behind her, seeking comfort in Matthew's presence. There he was, thank goodness, strong and solid on his horse, and she caught his gaze and held it for longer than was necessary, but she just couldn't seem to look away.

Everything would be fine, she told herself. For she loved that man, and he would take care of her. It was one certainty that she did not doubt.

CHAPTER 21

Matthew was unsure about what had transpired the previous day between Juliana and Lord Hemingway, but the earl obviously was not happy. He hadn't been able to set aside his breeding, for he had still helped Lady Juliana down from his phaeton, but he hadn't seemed particularly pleased about it, and after she was inside the house he stormed off without speaking to anyone else.

Matthew didn't hear any more of it, of course, until he arrived the next day to accompany Juliana on the errand she had requested him for. Jameson allowed him entrance with a somewhat uneasy expression, the reason for which Matthew soon discovered.

As he entered the foyer, he could hear the dowager duchess' voice ringing through the halls. He took Jameson's suggestion to wait in the foyer until Juliana was ready, but she and her mother must have been conversing in the front parlor, for he could hear each word very clearly.

"Do you know how much shame you are bringing upon us? Why, I wonder if Lady Hemingway will ever speak to me again. How could you, Juliana?"

"Mother, I do not love him. I could not marry him, and it was better that I told him as soon as I knew rather than waiting any longer."

"It already went on long enough!"

"Yes, but I didn't know then that I needed love for a marriage."

"Since when?"

"Since... I'm not sure, I suppose since I realized that I would never be able to love Lord Hemingway."

"He would have been good to you, Juliana." Her mother said, her voice losing its edge and becoming defeated. "No one is ever going to marry you now."

"You don't know that."

There was a pause, and Matthew knew that he should likely leave, that it was not his place to listen to their conversation. But he couldn't make his feet move.

"There is someone who will marry me. I know there is."

"I hope you don't believe it is that man."

"What man?" Juliana asked in a measured tone.

"The detective," her mother said, scorn in her voice. "I've seen the way you look at him, Juliana, the way he pines for you. I told Giles that he needed to find someone else to watch over you, but he assured me that Mr. Archibald was the utmost professional and that I was being ridiculous. Am I? Am I, Juliana?"

There was another pause, and Matthew wished he could see Juliana in this moment.

"I love him, Mother," she said quietly, and Matthew's heart swelled even as he knew Juliana had likely just destroyed any chance they ever had.

He waited for the dowager duchess to become upset all over again, but instead she took a different tactic.

"You think you love him, Juliana," she said, so softly that Matthew nearly didn't hear the words. "But it is simply an infatuation. The love will fade, and what then? You will be left taking care of a house that is half the size of this parlor, likely with four or five children, and no one to help you. Is that the life you want? Of wife and housemaid yourself? Love sounds all well and good, but would you give up all of this for a man? Do you know how many people would do anything to be in your place, Juliana? I'll tell you – all of England would. Think about that. Think long and hard."

Footsteps sounded in the hall, and Matthew inched around the wall to ensure that the dowager duchess would not see him. That was the last thing he needed.

It seemed, however, he had not been surreptitious enough.

"Mr. Archibald?"

He let out a breath as he stepped around the corner to face the woman who was half his size but, as much as he hated to admit it, twice as powerful.

"Yes, Your Grace?"

She eyed him with a piercing stare. "You know as well as I do that this will never work. Do not allow her to ruin her life. Do the right thing."

With a whirl of skirts, she was gone with a flourish, and Matthew stared after her as Juliana appeared in the hall.

"Matthew!" she cried, running to him without censure, throwing herself in his arms, and he instinctively wrapped them around her, covering her hair with his hand.

"Jules," he whispered into her ear, even as his heart broke slightly at the truth of what the dowager duchess had said. There was no right answer in all of this, that he knew. He just wasn't certain whether or not he could give Juliana up.

"Can we go?" she asked.

"Of course," he said, slowly letting her go. "Where are we going?"

"The printers," she said in a loud whisper with a flash in

her eyes, and he smiled, glad that she was seeing at least one of her dreams coming to fruition.

She gathered all she needed, including Abigail, and then they left, Matthew climbing atop the carriage as he always did, which gave him some time to gather his thoughts after all he had just heard.

The more he thought about it, the more he was convinced that the dowager duchess was right. It was everything he already knew, everything that he had told himself and Juliana, but he had allowed Juliana and his love for her to overcome those nagging thoughts.

They arrived at the shop that Juliana had selected, and he followed her in, standing to the side as he allowed her to speak to the printer alone, not wanting to interfere. He was impressed as she managed to negotiate a rather reasonable price, and she made a plan for distribution of the pamphlets as well. Her eyes shone when they left, and he wished that he didn't have to bring all her joy to a halt, but he did need to speak to her.

"When we reach Mayfair, would you like to walk for a time?"

"I would love to," she said, although there was some question in her eyes, but it would have to wait. When they reached the edge of her neighborhood, he had James stop the carriage and he helped Juliana out, while Abigail sat up top where she could watch them.

Juliana slipped her arm through Matthew's, and it felt so natural that he couldn't help but hold it close against him, taking all he could from this time together while he wondered how much longer they would have with one another.

"How much of the conversation with my mother did you hear?" she asked, immediately aware of what he wanted to discuss.

"Most of it, I would think."

"I am so sorry, Matthew. I—"

He had to stop her. "Juliana, you shouldn't have told Lord Hemingway you wouldn't marry him."

"Whyever not?" she said, stopping their forward progress. "I cannot marry him. I don't love him. Not the way I love you."

He closed his eyes as her words brought so much joy and yet so much pain. "Juliana, your mother is right. I cannot provide you with the life that you deserve."

"It has nothing to do with what I *deserve*," she said hotly. "I can choose the life I want, and, if you will have me, I want you."

"You are the sister of a duke."

"I am a woman."

She was making this very difficult for him.

"Juliana—"

"Please do not make decisions for me, Matthew. We said we would see where this takes us. Let us do that, at least, without allowing my mother to make the decision for us. Do you really believe me so shallow that I would give up the man I love for the grandeur of life?"

"I—"

They had started walking, and already Warwick House was looming in the distance. Matthew opened his mouth to respond, but a creature started running toward them, one he soon recognized as a dog.

"Lucy!" Juliana cried as she bent and picked up the dog – the dirty, mangy dog – in her arms, likely ruining the beautiful morning gown she wore. "Were you waiting for me? I am so sorry that I have no scraps with me."

She walked with the dog, speaking to it the whole time, as Matthew watched her go, wondering what the hell he was supposed to do about all of this.

THE SECRET OF THE DASHING DETECTIVE

* * *

JULIANA UNDERSTOOD MATTHEW'S CONCERN. She understood her mother's concern. She understood her own concerns. She just wasn't sure how to determine which were most valid.

She was hoping Emma could help her settle her feelings, and when her friend came to visit her room as they prepared for a ball that evening, she couldn't help but unburden the entirety of the dilemma upon her.

Emma listened, wide-eyed and interested, as Juliana told her entire tale, sitting in that regal way of hers until Juliana had run out of words.

"Well," she said, blinking at the end. "That is quite a conundrum."

"It is," Juliana said, sighing as she threw herself dramatically back on the bed.

"I did tell you from the start Mr. Archibald was handsome," Emma said, her eyes crinkling.

"It's not just that," Juliana said, unable to see the humor at this time. "He is kind and considerate, and he supports my dream and has never once made me feel foolish over what I am fighting for."

"What does he think about it all? What does he *feel* for you?"

Juliana hesitated. "I think he loves me. He has never said so, although he has told me that he cares for me. But he is hesitant in going forward, as he believes that perhaps my mother is right – that I would soon regret giving up my life for him."

Emma nodded wisely. "I do have to ask – would you? Would you be fine with living a life without servants, without fine dresses, with having to cook and clean and be the only caregiver for your children?"

Juliana's back stiffened. "I would actually enjoy looking after my children myself, I believe. As for everything else, I would have to learn. And you never know, Giles might provide me with enough dowry to hire a maid."

She managed a small smile, but Emma bit her lip, obviously uncertain as to whether Giles would go that far.

"I'm not sure what Giles would think of it, although he does like Mr. Archibald, and he does understand what it means to marry for love," Emma said slowly. "I cannot say for certain what he would think of you marrying outside of society, of likely moving away from Mayfair. He can hardly stand the thought of you walking around Mayfair without a man to look after your wellbeing. It is difficult to imagine the thought of you living a life that would put you in potentially more danger."

Juliana hadn't considered that aspect – but then, she would be with Matthew, and one thing she knew for certain was that he would always watch out for her. She just hoped that he didn't allow any ridiculous notions into his head about what that meant.

CHAPTER 22

Matthew stayed back as he watched the carriage continue up the drive to the large conservatory where this ball was being held. He couldn't stop himself from comparing the glamorous event in front of him with the gatherings that were held within his family. He preferred the comfort and love that he was used to, of course, but would Juliana? He had no idea.

He watched her emerge from the carriage, saw her look back at him, watched her mother follow her gaze and scowl at him before they continued inside.

The duke emerged last and walked over to Matthew before he escorted his wife in.

"There is going to be a large crowd tonight, so I would prefer that you remained inside to keep an eye on Juliana. I don't think they would allow anyone in who doesn't belong here, but as you have said, we cannot be convinced that whoever took her before is not of society. I will speak to the host."

Matthew nodded and followed in behind, knowing that Owen and a couple of his other men were also placed outside the doors of the venue. He was allowed in the front door but then directed to follow a different path into the ballroom where the dancing would be held. When he emerged, he found himself at the side of the room where a line of footmen stood, ready to answer the whims of all the nobility.

He was being treated as a servant. Which wasn't surprising, yet still, it did nothing but deepen the chasm between him and Juliana. He did as the duke had asked, keeping an eye on her throughout the night, which of course wasn't difficult as he couldn't help but watch her, wherever she went. She circled through the crowd, greeting her many friends and acquaintances, spending a great deal of time with Lady Maria and of course her sister and the duchess. She danced quite a few times, and Matthew had to tamp down the anger that simmered in his belly at other men with their hands upon her. He saw Lord Hemingway in attendance, but the man avoided Juliana, which he supposed was a blessing for all.

He then saw Juliana speak to her mother before exiting through the wide entrance of the room farther into the building, and he guessed she was going to the lady's room. He wasn't sure how he was supposed to shadow her there, but he also didn't like the idea of her wandering the halls alone. He looked one way and then the other, trying to determine the quickest way to follow her, but it seemed that would take him through the crowd, which he knew would never be allowed. Instead, he had to keep to the outskirts of the room, and by the time he made it through the doors to follow her down, he had lost sight of her. He looked one way and then the other, trying to find which room she had entered.

He opened a couple of doors, once finding a couple in a tryst, another time finding a woman sitting alone who seemed none too pleased to see him. He muttered his apologies as he started to panic slightly that he couldn't catch sight of Juliana. Finally, he thought he heard a voice down the hall – until he realized that it was actually a shout.

"Let me go, you lout!"

There was a grunt and Matthew rushed down the hall, turning the corner only to collide with a figure. A very familiar figure. He reached out his arms to catch Juliana in them before she fell, looking past her to see a gentleman leaning against the wall, holding his arms against his stomach.

"What happened?" he asked, torn between wanting to ensure Juliana's well-being and going after the man – even if he was a peer.

"This is Lord Dennison. We seemed to have had a *misunderstanding*," she said through gritted teeth. "Fortunately, I had enough knowledge of how to make it quite clear that I did not welcome his advances."

"You have it all wrong," the man huffed as he reached toward her in supplication.

"I assure you I do not," she said, before tugging on Matthew's arm to lead him away.

Matthew tamped down his innate need to shove his fist into the man's face, knowing it be Juliana's ruin if he did so.

He couldn't, however, help the sick ball of tension that began to churn in his stomach. Juliana had been in danger – perhaps not the danger he had been worried about, but danger nonetheless. And he hadn't been there in time to stop it, because he had been standing against the wall like a servant. How would it be any different if they were living in Holborn and he had to leave her alone when he went to work? He couldn't spend every minute of his life looking after her to keep her safe. And nor could he afford for someone to watch her at all times.

He was caught between needing to track her every move

and to leave her in the hands of someone else entirely, knowing that he was just going to make the inevitable all the worse.

He watched her return to the ballroom, so intent on tracking her that he didn't notice anyone approaching him until he felt the tug on his elbow.

"Matthew."

He whirled around to find Owen standing behind him, a look on his face that Matthew recognized well.

"What is it? What's wrong?"

"We were watching the doors and we saw a familiar figure. Dr. Lewis. We have him waiting outside. He claims he is here to see a patient, but we also found his mother nearby."

Matthew's heart sank. He had been certain of Lewis' innocence, intent that he would have nothing to do with the duke's demise, for his own sake as well as Juliana's. She had been so pleased to meet her half-brother that he dreaded the thought of having to tell her that he might not be as innocent as he had seemed.

"Very well. I'll go speak with him to determine if it is as he says."

"I'm coming with you."

Matthew turned to find the duke standing there, his face hardened.

"Your Grace," he said, "did you hear what Mr. Green discovered?"

"I heard enough. Lewis is behind this, then?"

"We do not know that. We only know that he is here tonight. He is waiting outside."

"Let us go, then."

"Owen, will you stay inside and watch Lady Juliana?"

Owen nodded as Matthew and the duke walked through the ballroom – apparently, he was allowed if a duke made it so – to the front of the building.

THE SECRET OF THE DASHING DETECTIVE

"Where is he?"

"Owen said by one of the doors. I would assume a back door. Your Grace, we do not know—"

"But we will soon."

They rounded the corner and there was Lewis standing, bag in hand, by the back door. His mother stood beside him, arms crossed over her chest.

"Archibald. Your Grace." Lewis greeted them, his tone as calm as ever, although there was a hint of unease within it.

"This is it, then?" The duke said, his anger already growing. "Your apparent need to know your siblings was only to get close to us? To try to come after us from the inside?"

"Pardon me?" Lewis said, his spine straightening as he rose to his full height, which was near to the same as the duke's.

"That's why you're here, to come after one of us again? Was your mother acting lookout?"

"I am here as his assistant," his mother said, her eyes bright.

"His assistant?" The duke scoffed. "Now I have heard it all."

"As it happens, my mother does assist me in my work," Lewis said, his tone even, but there was an edge to it now. "I was called here this evening."

"Did a young lady hurt her feet from dancing too much?" the duke asked, obviously convinced now that Lewis was behind all of this.

"I will not share the condition of a patient with you, but I do request that you allow me to enter the conservatory to offer my help."

"To go in after my family? No. You can enter once we leave."

Matthew looked from one of them to the other, knowing that the duke was trying to do what he thought was right to protect those he loved, but Matthew's instincts told him that the duke's judgement was clouded in this regard.

"Your Grace," he murmured. "Perhaps I could accompany Dr. Lewis inside. We would not want anyone requiring his help to suffer unnecessarily."

The duke tapped his foot in uncertainty, finally piercing Matthew with his stare.

"Fine. But if anything happens, it is on you. I am going to take my family home."

"Very well," Matthew said. "I understand."

Dr. Lewis walked past the duke without another word, their shoulders clipping as they passed one another, his mother following behind him after sending a dark glare the duke's way.

They went not to the ballroom, but to the room where Matthew had seen the young woman alone. They entered, and Lewis went over to speak softly with her. He nodded, then returned to the door and spoke in a low voice to Matthew.

"Would you remain outside the door for privacy? I believe it is not too great of an ailment, but she does require some examination."

"Very well," Matthew said, stepping out of the room and closing the door behind him, leaning his head back against it. He was inclined to believe Lewis, but then, he was perhaps allowing his own preference for the man to cause a bias. The duke seemed much more convinced that he was in the wrong, and he was the one who paid him for his trouble.

After a few minutes, there was a knock on the door, and Lewis exited, leaving his mother behind with the girl.

"She will be fine," he said. "As for what has transpired here tonight, I cannot pretend not to be greatly disappointed. It does, however, make one thing clear to me."

"Which is?"

"It does not matter that we share blood, nor a desire to come to know one another better. I will always be a physician, a bastard, and not worthy of the family's time. They can say all they want about having a desire to know me better, that they would accept me as part of their family, but that is all it is – words. It is actions that show the true nature of the person, and look how easily I was suspected, simply by my presence here. It is a shame, truly, for I would have liked to have siblings."

His mother emerged then, her face stony as Lewis nodded at her. "Let us go, Mother."

Matthew started down the hallway with them, and Lewis turned to him. "There is no need to follow us home. I can assure you that I am not going after the duke, nor his family. In fact, I will have nothing further to do with them."

Matthew watched him go before realizing there was nothing further for him here. He gathered his horse from the stable and rode to Mayfair, stopping in front of Warwick House. He conversed with the stablemaster, ensured that the entire Remington family had made it home, and then continued on to his own boarding house in Holborn. There, he looked around him, at all of the changes Juliana had made. He could sense her presence, and he yearned for her to be here with him, but he also knew that was simply wishful thinking. She was home in Mayfair, where she belonged. Now he just had to make that clear to her.

For Lewis was right. As much as she said that she loved him, that they would make it work, those were just words. She would never truly be happy with him, as much as she tried to tell herself she would be.

It was all just a dream.

CHAPTER 23

Juliana paced the drawing room, waiting for Matthew to arrive. She knew that he would be here soon – she had heard Giles ask Jameson to send a note, asking for him to come meet with him. Giles, apparently, was convinced that their half-brother was behind all of their family's dangers.

Juliana tried to tell him that he was wrong, that there was no way that Dr. Lewis could have done this, that he likely was truly treating a patient, but Giles told her not to be so naïve, that she was only believing what she wanted to believe.

But she would believe in Matthew. He would know the truth. She was sure of it.

She heard Matthew enter and Jameson lead him into Giles' study. She raced to the parlor next to his study, pressing her ear against the wall to listen to the exchange as best she could. The walls were sturdy and well-built so she couldn't hear the entirety of the conversation, but she did hear Giles tell Matthew he was certain that Lewis was behind all of this.

Matthew did not appear to agree, but Giles was convinced. Juliana took a deep breath, hoping that Matthew could make Giles see reason.

But then she heard Giles' next words very clearly – ones that hurt her deep within her soul – "we will no longer require your services."

Giles was nice about it, thanking Matthew and telling him that he appreciated all that he had done for the family. Juliana could only imagine what Matthew was thinking, likely allowing the guilt to creep in over what had happened between them. But Juliana refused to allow herself to be affected by that. For this was no passing fling. She loved Matthew Archibald, and she was going to tell him so again, as many times as he needed to hear it to understand that she wasn't leaving him for anything. She was convinced now – she could accept whatever life awaited her, as long as they were side by side

For the thought of being without him – of him walking out of her life when he left the employ of her family – was too frightful to bear.

She heard the door of Giles' study open, and she kept to the side as she watched Matthew exit. Fortunately, Giles didn't walk him out, and once he was out of Giles' eyesight, she followed him down the hallway.

"Matthew!" she called when she saw no one else about, and the look on his face when he turned was enough to nearly break her heart, although why he would feel such a way, she had no idea. He wasn't leaving her – just the job.

He stopped, waiting for her, but he didn't stretch out his arms nor smile nor give any sign that he was particularly pleased to see her.

"Your brother is convinced that Lewis and his mother are behind everything," he said, his voice flat. "He wants to take action against them."

"You don't believe that is true, do you?"

"I do not," he said, shaking his head. "But His Grace is convinced."

"I will talk to him," Juliana said with determination. "He will change his mind. He just so desperately wants this all to be over."

"He has decided that you no longer need protection," Matthew said, his brows creasing together. "But I do ask you to be careful, Juliana. Keep your knife with you, even if it seems ridiculous. Do not go anywhere alone – take someone else besides Abigail with you. Have at least three or four people with you everywhere you go, even if that includes footmen. I will try to have Owen watch out for you when he can."

Juliana's confusion grew the more Matthew spoke.

"But... what about you?"

"I am no longer in your brother's employ."

"Yes, but surely the two of us will still see one another?"

His lips pursed together.

"Perhaps we should walk in the gardens."

"Very well," Juliana said, her heart beating hard at the expression on Matthew's face. She didn't like where this was going. She didn't like it at all.

She found her bonnet and the two of them walked outdoors, not earning any cursory glances from the servants, for none of them yet knew that Matthew had been dismissed.

Once they were out of view from the house, Matthew took a great intake of breath and turned to Juliana, his expression unreadable.

"Juliana, I need you to know how much I care for you."

"I care for you as well. In fact, I love you," she emphasized, needing him to understand how true her words were.

"I am a lucky man to deserve even a hint of your affection," he said, his hands behind his back when she wished that they were outstretched toward her, around her body, anywhere but kept away from her. "And, in fact, I have taken too much of it. I have allowed this to go on for far too long."

"What are you talking about?" she asked in growing panic, tilting her head to the side.

"This is goodbye, Juliana," he said softly. "This is not a world in which the two of us can be together."

It took a moment for his words to sink in, for her to understand exactly what he was saying.

"How can you say that?" she protested, her pain emerging as anger as she lashed out, striking his chest. "That is not for you to decide."

"It is for both of us to decide," he said, and she hated how stoic he was, standing there staring at her. "I cannot provide you with the life you deserve."

She stepped closer to him, needing him to understand. "It is not a particular *life* I want, Matthew. It is *you*. I don't care what comes with it. I want to live my life by your side, in whatever way that means."

"You do not know what you are saying."

"I do!" she exclaimed. "I have seen where you live, what your family is like. I enjoy my time with them. I have no qualms about taking care of a house. I will have much to learn, yes, but I am willing and capable."

"What if, at some point, you decide you are no longer happy with the arrangement? You will be stuck, for the rest of your life."

"How can you tell me what I would feel? I thought you understood better than any other man that I have a right to think and feel as I choose."

"I know you are perfectly capable of doing so, Juliana, but you are young and—"

She scoffed at that, annoyed that he would think so little of her and whether or not she would know her own mind.

"Plus," he continued, "have you ever considered what your mother would think of the match? Or your brother? If your family refuses to acknowledge our union they may no longer welcome your presence in their home."

That took Juliana aback for a moment. He was right – she was well aware that her mother wouldn't approve of the two of them, but she had difficulty considering that any of her family members would refuse to speak to her again.

"We will figure it out. Together," she said earnestly, but he just sighed and shook his head.

"I don't think it is the best of ideas, Juliana."

"The *best of ideas?*" she repeated. "How can you put it so casually? We are talking about our lives. Our love!"

He looked off into the distance before returning his gaze to her, and this time, he simply looked sad, which was almost worse. "Last night, Lewis was judged simply for being in a particular place at the wrong time. The entire building was full of the peerage, but none of them were under suspicion. Yet here comes a man who, despite how hard he has worked for his current status, is still seen as less than in the eyes of those who apparently matter. This is a man who has the blood of a duke within him. How do you think your family would ever see me? How do you think you wouldn't eventually come to resent me?"

The pain had receded, and Juliana's anger was growing by the moment.

"I cannot believe you think such little of me," she said, stepping toward him, and he backed up just a step so that she was not standing on his toes. "That you would think I am so shallow that I need all of the fineries in life or care what everyone else thinks. I have told you time and again what I want, but it seems that you do not care any more than anyone else in my life. This is what you want? A life without me? Fine, then. So be it. If you cannot fight for me, for what is between us, then I shall quit doing all of the loving and all of the fighting for both of us. You only made me look the fool. Goodbye, Matthew. Enjoy your life."

With that, she turned and stormed away, hands in fists, before he could see the tears that had started to stream out of her eyes. She waited for him to call out to her, to tell her that he had been wrong, but it seemed that he had no wish to care what she felt or how she was doing.

She would just have to accept the fact that he simply didn't want her.

CHAPTER 24

Matthew returned to Holborn with purpose. He was done with the Warwick family and Mayfair and all that it represented. He didn't belong there, and neither did Juliana belong here with him.

This was how it should be, he continued to repeat to himself. He had made the right decision.

So why did it feel so awful? All he could picture was her face in front of him, stricken, panicked, to be replaced by so much anger.

At least the anger was better than the pain he had initially seen written there. Pain that he had caused. For so long, he had done everything to be the one to protect her from threats that might bring her anything but joy.

Now he had hurt her worse than anyone ever had before.

He had known better, he berated himself as he kicked at a large stone in the middle of the street. He should have stopped this before it had started, should never have let her in.

And yet he knew, deep within him, that there was no way he could ever have prevented her from getting wedged into his heart. She was the woman for him. Even if they couldn't be together, he knew that he would never love another the way he loved her.

But this was for the best.

The ball had made it clear to him where his place was in society, and where she stood. His job had been to protect her, not to fall in love with her. She had been raised to attend dances and sew needlepoint, not to be the wife of an investigator. Meanwhile he would never be accepted as her husband, which would mean a life away from all she had ever known.

Better to finish this before it went any further than it already had.

He slammed open the door of his office, nodding to his men before standing at the front of the room.

"We're off the Warwick case," he said. "The duke considers it finished."

There was a clamor among the five or so men who sat in the room as they all began hurling questions at him. Matthew held up a hand.

"The duke believes that Lewis and his mother were behind it all, and he said that he is going to take it from here."

"There is no way it was Lewis," Owen said, standing with concern and walking over to Matthew, obviously gathering there was more to the story, but Matthew held up a hand.

"I agree with you. I don't believe it is him either, which I told the duke. But if this is what the man wants, there is nothing else we can do. We have more cases awaiting us. I just have to go through some files and determine what case we take next. Take the night off, men, you are relieved of your duties for today."

They all lost their questions at that, filing out through the door, although Owen remained behind, following Matthew into his office.

"The duke wouldn't see reason, then?"

"No," Matthew said, shaking his head. "I sense that he likely isn't pleased about the entire situation of having a brother, of what it might mean or what it says about his family. He was quick to jump on the certainty of Lewis' involvement."

"What else?"

"What do you mean?"

"What else happened?"

"Nothing."

Owen snorted. "Don't give me that. You look like one of Lady Juliana's forlorn puppies."

Matthew started at Juliana's name, unsuccessfully attempting to hide his reaction from Owen.

"Lady Juliana and I became close while I was looking after her. When I left, she… wasn't pleased."

Owen looked at him closely, finally leaning down to stare right into Matthew's eyes.

"Can you get out of my face?" Matthew asked him.

"You love her."

"I do not."

"You do!" Owen crowed. "And, let me guess, you told her that you couldn't be together, that you are star-crossed lovers, and she's too good for you?"

Defeated, Matthew heaved a sigh. "Something like that."

"Oh, Matthew," Owen said, shaking his head. "Sometimes I am not certain what to do with you."

"There is nothing to do."

"Why are you sitting here then, looking like the entire world is against you?"

"Well," Matthew said, deciding the truth was the best policy, "Lady Juliana hates me now, as I'm sure does Dr. Lewis, who was becoming something of a friend. Let us just say that it has all put me in a mood that is not my best."

"There might not be anything you can do about the lady at the moment," Owen said thoughtfully, "but perhaps you can make things right with the doctor. He seems a reasonable man. Just explain your stance to him."

Matthew looked up at Owen. Damn it, but he was right.

"I can, Owen," he said, rising from his desk. "Come, he isn't far."

"I'm not going with you," Owen said, shaking his head. "I'm just telling you that it's a good idea."

"Fine," Matthew said with a sigh. "Don't help me then."

Matthew could hear Owen's laugh as he continued out the door, likely home to his family.

But Matthew knew he was right – he had to talk to Lewis, to let him know that he, at least, believed in him. Lewis was a good man and was owed that.

Matthew locked the door behind him and continued the few blocks down to Lewis' home. It was actually amazing that he hadn't come to know him sooner, being that their lives were physically so close together.

He arrived just as another person did, and he waited while Lewis addressed the issue. The waiting gave him time to think of the situation with Juliana – not that he wanted to do so, but he couldn't much help it. He figured she would be on his mind for some time. He had no idea how to rid it of her.

When Lewis finally appeared, he gave Matthew a measured nod before motioning him back to his study. Matthew could understand his reluctance and felt a bit like a child waiting to be chastised.

"I must offer you my apologies again, it seems," Matthew said, taking a chair before Lewis could say anything. "I hadn't given my men any new information to tell them not to detain you if they were to see you anywhere. Although I must tell you that I did everything in my power to convince the duke you had nothing to do with the entirety of the situation. It seems he doesn't place much trust in what I say anymore, however, for he has told me that he is now finished with my services."

"I see," Lewis said, sitting back in his chair, the tight grip he held on the edges the only sign he was affected. "Well, I cannot say I am surprised. It is the way of the nobility, is it not?"

"I suppose it is," Matthew responded. "I had thought some of them were different – including the Remington family – but then maybe I was foolish to expect it."

"What of the Lady Juliana?" Lewis asked, obviously rather perceptive.

"We have parted ways as well," Matthew said abruptly, not wishing to speak any further of her or what had happened between the two of them. Lewis seemed to understand as he simply nodded.

"Perhaps I am the one who will now be requiring your services."

"How so?"

"If the duke decides to prosecute me, I am going to need some help. From a solicitor yes, but perhaps from an investigator as well should I need help proving my innocence."

Matthew cursed under his breath.

"Let us hope he comes to his senses before it gets that far. At his core, I know the duke is a good man. Perhaps if it is his family he is concerned about, it is his family we must speak to."

Lewis opened his hands in front of him. "I'm all ears."

* * *

JULIANA KNEW BETTER than to go outside the fence surrounding Warwick House by herself, but she would have

THE SECRET OF THE DASHING DETECTIVE

given anything at that moment to have Lucy cuddled on her lap instead of licking her hand through the fence.

"It was terrible, Lucy, truly it was," she said to the dog, who tilted her head to the side and twitched one ear as she listened to Juliana's tale. "He's a stubborn-headed mule, and I finally realized that there was no chance of ever making him see reason. So I let him go. But it could have been the most foolish decision I have ever made for now I don't know if I will ever get him back."

"Sometimes letting something fly free is the only way to get it to return to you."

Juliana whipped her head around, shocked to find her grandmother standing behind her, walking stick held regally in her hand as she stood staring without comment at the dog Juliana petted.

"Grandmother," Juliana said, scrambling to her feet. "What are you doing out here?"

"Seeking you out," she said. "You barely ate anything this morning, and I wanted to see if you were all right or if you had fainted out here from hunger."

"I am fine."

"I am glad to hear it. That was my first concern. Secondly, I wanted you to see this. A lad was handing them out when I returned from visiting with Lady Tanningham."

She held out a stack of paper to Juliana – a stack of paper she recognized very well.

"My pamphlet!" she said excitedly, unable to contain the glee that broke through her melancholy. "That is to say, a—"

"There is no need to hide your secret from me, child. I am well aware of what you have been up to."

"But how—"

"Who did you think used that little parlor before you did? Did you ever wonder why it was so elegantly appointed that it would invite you as it has? I happened to find your work stored away in one of the drawers one day."

"I see," Juliana said, feeling foolish to have ever considered that she wouldn't be found out.

"Your ideas are peculiar," Lady Winchester said, never one to hide her true thoughts on a subject. "However, you have written in a concise, straightforward manner and some of your arguments have even convinced me that I could take a better path."

Juliana couldn't help but laugh at that. "Thank you, Grandmother."

"I tell only the truth. Now, come sit with your grandmother on a bench over near the pond so we can discuss what has happened with this young jackanape."

Juliana said farewell to Lucy before following after her grandmother, wondering if the woman even needed her walking stick with how fast she walked, or if it was all simply for show. She guessed she would likely never know the truth.

"There is nothing to tell, really," Juliana said as she sat next to her grandmother and watched the few birds who were using the shallow water as their pool. "I love him and he doesn't want to be with me."

"You *love* him?" Lady Winchester's eyebrows rose. "That is quite a statement. Are you certain of it?"

"Absolutely," Juliana said with determination. "Although I am quite cross with him at the moment."

Her grandmother chuckled. "It cannot always be sunshine."

"That is most certainly the truth."

"I am assuming his objection is the difference in your stations."

"Yes."

"He is not wrong. If you were to marry him – an investigator from Holborn – your life would never be the same."

Juliana looked down at her hands, which were twisted in the fine muslin of her skirts. "My life will never be the same regardless. Not now that I have met him."

Her grandmother studied her for so long that Juliana could feel the time passing.

"You truly do love him."

"I do."

"And you are willing to give up all of this," she waved her walking stick over the gardens in front of her, "for a life with him?"

"I am."

"Well, then," her grandmother said with a shrug that made it seem like it was so simple, "you have to make him believe you."

"How?"

Her grandmother grinned wryly at her.

"That is a question that only you can answer."

CHAPTER 25

*J*uliana waited nervously in front of the door. Despite the family's friendliness, she had no idea how she was now going to be received. She looked back at the carriage, where Emma smiled encouragingly at her, Prudence watching somewhat skeptically.

As she had promised Matthew, Juliana had ensured that she didn't travel alone. If all went according to plan, she would remain with Abigail, a footman, and whoever agreed to help her with her scheme.

If it didn't? Well, then, she would be going home with the other women before she could even attempt to change Matthew's mind.

Matthew's mother opened the door, surprise in her eyes when she saw who was on the other side.

"Lady Juliana!" she exclaimed. "It is lovely to see you, but I must ask – what are you doing here?"

"I have come for your help, actually," she said. "You see, I must convince Matthew that I am willing to start a life with him – however or wherever that might be. Matthew doesn't trust what I have told him to be true, and at first I wasn't sure how to assure him, but I have an idea. I just need your help – and a little advice."

Mrs. Archibald didn't say anything at first. She just looked Juliana up and down. Juliana had taken care to dress respectably but not too ostensibly, which she was particularly glad of at the moment.

"Of course, dear," Mrs. Archibald finally said with a warm smile, opening the door wider to allow Juliana entrance into the house. Juliana waved at Emma and Prudence, who heartily returned it. She had a feeling that they were more optimistic of this entire plan than she was, but she had to do something to at least try – even if it would lead to nothing but a ruined dinner. Which was fine. At least she would have done something to prove herself.

He didn't think she could ever live in a house like this? He was wrong. She just needed him to believe what she was telling him. And he always said actions were stronger than words.

"Come sit," Matthew's mother said, waving her to the couch. "Tell me what my son did."

"Well," Juliana said, her eyes on her hands as she lowered herself into the seat, "he told me that we could never be together. That it would never work between us. I have tried to convince him that I would be with him no matter what it takes. He just doesn't believe me."

Matthew's mother waited a moment before replying.

"My son is very stubborn," she said, to which Juliana nodded heartily.

"I know."

His mother smiled the fond smile that only a mother can when considering her own child's potential shortcomings. "But that means that once he commits, he is loyal to a fault and would always prefer to see something through. If he feels the same for you as you do for him – and, after seeing the two of you together, I suspect he does – then he will come around. He just needs to realize the truth of your words first."

Juliana nodded, agreeing with all that Mrs. Archibald said. Then she replied, "I was thinking of cooking him dinner. There is just one problem – I do not know how."

At that, Mrs. Archibald dissolved into laughter, but she soon let it fade and patted Juliana's arm encouragingly.

"Not to worry, dear. That, we can help with. Now, before we start, let us gather Betsy and Mary."

Mrs. Archibald set off to find her daughters while Juliana began writing out what she had noticed Matthew had enjoyed the few times they had eaten together.

She would prove she could make a home for the two of them. And then it would be up to him whether or not he wanted to believe in her. If, even after that, he refused to do so, if he wouldn't believe in her or her love? Well, then, he wasn't the man for her. The words stung even as they raced through her mind, but she refused to allow anyone to make her feel less than she was.

Not even Matthew.

Not long after Matthew's mother had departed, she returned with her daughters in tow, who seemed ecstatic that Juliana had arrived.

"Matthew is a stubborn-headed mule," Betsy said, sitting down and crossing her arms over her chest. Juliana couldn't help but laugh at that.

"I was saying the exact thing myself to someone else not long ago, actually," she said, although she didn't mention that she had been speaking to a dog.

"I've made a list of what I think Matthew would enjoy, although I would appreciate any recommendations you have to offer, for you would all know much better than I would what he might like."

She held out the list, which Betsy and Mary took and began to read, heads together as they poured over it.

"You have come to know him well," Betsy said, looking up at Juliana with eyes so like Matthew's that it was oddly unsettling.

"I am observant," Juliana said, although the heat rushed to her cheeks, for she knew that she was mostly observant of Matthew and his preferences.

"There is only one thing I would change," Betsy said.

"Which is?"

"Matthew has not been eating meat as of late."

Juliana was struck speechless for a moment. "He... hasn't?"

"No," Betsy said, a smile growing on her face, Mary's matching hers. "It seems your arguments have made quite the impression on him."

"But I haven't pressed any arguments on him at all," Juliana said, sitting back on the couch, dumbfounded. "The only way he would know is... well, I suppose it must be from my pamphlet."

"Your pamphlet?"

Juliana quickly explained what she had been working on. "Matthew supplied some of the drawings for it."

Now it was his sisters' turn to be without words.

"Matthew hasn't drawn or painted in ages," Mary finally said. "He said he was too busy, that he had far too much else to do. We thought it such a pity, for he is so talented. It seems that you have brought out the best in him, Lady Juliana."

"Please, just call me Juliana," Juliana insisted. It seemed silly to use her title when she was trying to prove that she was prepared for this lifestyle.

The sisters exchanged a look. "Very well."

"When would you like to do this?" Betsy asked.

"Is tomorrow too soon? If you could help guide me as to

what to purchase, I can go into the market and find everything."

"We can do that for you," Mary said quickly, but Juliana was already shaking her head.

"No. I must do this myself. Although... perhaps your accompaniment would be lovely."

She wasn't fool enough to think that she wouldn't require some advice on where to go and what to do.

They settled everything and walked Juliana to the door, where James had returned to wait for her. Betsy reached out and squeezed her hand.

"Try not to worry. All will be fine."

"Thank you," she said with a reassuring smile before she left the comfort of Matthew's childhood home. As she greeted James, who helped her into the carriage, she knew one thing – she was making the right decision. She had to fight for Matthew – or she might forever regret it.

* * *

THE NEXT DAY, Matthew suddenly found himself overwhelmed with nothing to do and a great need to fill his time. For he was miserable. All he could think of was Juliana. He was contriving reasons in his mind for why he had to go see her, knowing he was acting a fool but unable to stop himself. For this was all his own doing. He knew that. He could have her in his arms right now if he chose to – but he couldn't do that to her. He couldn't upend her entire life, couldn't be selfish enough to reach for the one woman who was far too good for him.

He would have liked to have tried to distract himself with work, but the new cases he had decided upon had not yet started. The Smithfield case had ended long ago, when they had determined that the wife wasn't being unfaithful — she had simply taken up a new hobby, one she didn't think her husband would approve of. He was waiting to meet with a man the next day to resolve his requirements, and it was yet to be determined if the other had resolved itself.

Finally, Matthew convinced himself that it was the perfect day for him to go speak to the Duchess of Warwick and the ladies Juliana and Prudence to see if he could convince them to intervene on Dr. Lewis' behalf. Which was the *only* reason he was returning to Warwick House, he sternly reminded himself. It had nothing to do with his wish to see Juliana.

Once he ascertained whether they could aid him in his quest, he would determine how to best prove Lewis' innocence. He already knew that Lewis had an alibi for the night Juliana had been taken, but it was his mother, which the duke insisted was no alibi at all. Instead, Matthew would have to make it clear that Lewis had known nothing of his own father or background besides the fact he had not been present in his life. For that, he would need Mrs. Lewis' help, but he would take it one step at a time and see what he could do on his own before involving her.

His horse seemed to know the way to Warwick House without Matthew having to guide him there, and soon enough he was staring up at the gate that led through to the grounds behind. He was just about to go through when he heard a sharp yap next to him, and he looked down to find Juliana's little Lucy staring up at him.

"How are you, girl?" he asked, to which Lucy responded with a quick bark. "Is something the matter?"

He was talking to a dog. Ridiculous. But he couldn't help that Juliana and her love for the animals seemed to have touched something inside of him, and he was finding himself more and more curious about her opinions on their right to have better welfare. If nothing else, spending time watching

Juliana and Lucy together had proven that a bond could certainly exist between human and animal.

Just thinking of it, however, had him missing Juliana all over again, although he would be seeing her soon enough. He just wasn't sure what kind of reception he would receive.

He rode in through the gates, leaving his horse with a groom before taking to the steps. Jameson seemed considerably surprised to see him.

"Mr. Archibald," he said. "I was not expecting you."

It was interesting how butlers could say so much with so few words.

"I am here to speak with the ladies Juliana and Prudence and the duchess, if it is at all possible."

"I shall see if they are receiving callers," Jameson said, his reception frostier than it had been previously, that was for certain.

He returned not long afterward.

"The duchess and Lady Prudence will see you."

Matthew followed him along the corridor, wondering just what that meant. Had Juliana given up on him entirely?

He entered the drawing room, finding the duchess and Lady Prudence awaiting him on the sofa.

"Mr. Archibald," the duchess said, not belying any of her emotions toward him, although her tone was missing its usual friendly note. "Welcome. What can we do for you?"

"I am here to speak to you about Dr. Lewis," he said, taking the armchair across from them. "It seems His Grace is convinced of the man's guilt; however, I am quite certain that he has had no role in threatening your family. I was hoping that you, perhaps, could help him believe otherwise."

"You are asking me to go against my husband, and for Lady Prudence to go against her brother?" the duchess said with a raised eyebrow.

THE SECRET OF THE DASHING DETECTIVE

"I am only asking for help in convincing him of the truth," he tried instead.

To his surprise, the corners of the duchess' lips turned up slightly. "Very well. As it happens, we are inclined to agree with you. Giles is so eager to be finished with this threat that he is not thinking rationally about it. What can we do?"

He outlined his plan, asking them to slowly work away at the duke's arguments.

"I am afraid, however," he said, "that there is still someone out there waiting to find a weakness in your defenses. Please continue to be vigilant."

"Of course," they said, before rising in an indication it was time for his departure.

"Will you please... provide my regards to Lady Juliana?" he asked hesitatingly.

"Of course," the duchess said. "I believe she is currently visiting with Lady Maria."

"Is she now?" Matthew said as his heart started to beat more rapidly. He had a bad feeling about that – a very bad feeling.

If Juliana had provided such an excuse to her sister and her closest friend in the world, it was most likely she was not with Lady Maria, but rather on some mission or another – only this time, he was not there to look after her.

He strode toward the front entrance with new purpose – he had to find Juliana. It didn't matter whether or not they had a future together or what had been said between them. He was not going to let anything happen to her. Ever.

Which told him something had been sitting there, below the surface of his consciousness, that he hadn't yet accepted. She was as much a part of him as he was his own man, and he could see no future without her. Now he just had to decide if that pull to one another was enough to overcome all else that stood between them.

He already had one hand on the door when a voice behind him stopped him.

"Mr. Archibald."

He turned to find Lady Winchester standing there, staring at him with all the knowledge in the world held within her eyes.

"Yes?"

"I can tell you where to find Juliana, but on one condition."

"Yes?"

He waited for her to tell him that he would have to vow to never see her again, to not pursue any romance with her. But her words completely surprised him.

"You must not play the fool again."

CHAPTER 26

Juliana was quite proud of herself.

As she lifted the apron Mrs. Archibald had given her to wipe a bead of sweat off her forehead, she could admit that she was exhausted, yes. But this was rewarding work. She gripped the handle of the spoon and turned it slowly through the soup she had made – by herself. She had cooked the entirety of the meal, although she'd had some help in other regards.

Matthew's sisters had accompanied her to the marketplace and Juliana had done her very best not to appear completely out of place, although she had a feeling that she had utterly failed in that regard.

She was glad she had not been alone. When she had reached into her small reticule to pay what the first vendor had asked of her, Betsy had placed her hand on top of hers to stop her.

"He is asking far too much from you," Betsy whispered in her ear. "He can tell from the finery of your clothes that you can afford to pay more. You should be paying half that. You have to bargain with him."

Juliana had bargained before – with the printer in order to get a better rate for the pamphlets, for example – but she wasn't prepared for haggling in the marketplace.

Fortunately, Betsy was quite adept and after Juliana's half-hearted attempts, she stepped in and gave an example of how it should be done.

Juliana did much better the second time around, and soon enough they had arms and baskets loaded with all that she needed and returned to Matthew's parents' house. His mother had suggested that their house would be the best place for Juliana to make the meal, for she had far better equipment than Matthew. She promised that she and her husband would remain scarce when Matthew arrived, although Juliana received the impression that she felt that perhaps the two of them would require some chaperoning. She wasn't entirely wrong, although Juliana had been rather looking forward to time completely alone with Matthew.

If all went right tonight, however, they would have the rest of their lives to make up for it.

Juliana stirred the soup, finding another spoon to test it. It tasted decent, but she was aware that there was something missing. She knew that her efforts in the kitchen would never rival those of their own cook, nor the women of Matthew's family, but she was determined to do this by herself. His sisters had left the house long ago, needing to return to their families, and Matthew's mother stopped in now and then to check on things. She had provided Juliana with the instructions that she needed, and then had left her to it.

The soup needed spice, she decided. She eyed the small space and the cupboards below, wondering if it would be impertinent for her to go looking for what she needed. She opened a few drawers and doors but felt like she was trespassing. She waited for Matthew's mother to return, but the house felt empty, as if she was entirely alone. The idea actually spooked her some, and she was more inclined to go out and find what she was looking for than to remain here alone. The market was just around the corner and all she needed was a quick dash of parsley.

Surely she could head out alone and find what she needed? She was in Holborn and no one knew she was here. There was no reason anyone would have followed her or have any idea who she truly was.

Giles didn't seem to feel there was a threat any longer, not now that he had decided that Dr. Lewis was at fault. While she wasn't inclined to agree with him, she didn't think she was in danger here and he no longer required her to have protection following her. She should have a chaperone, but how could a chaperone help if she were in any danger?

Besides, it wasn't as though she was going any long distance and Matthew was going to be here soon, if he promptly answered his mother's summons.

She hung her apron on the peg beside the door and checked on the soup before tentatively turning the knob. This was ridiculous, she told herself. She was a grown woman who had become afraid of her own shadow.

Filling herself with courage, she pushed through the door, walking down the street, turning the corner and starting through the market. The light was beginning to dim as the sun set on the dinner hour, hurrying her along as she must return before Matthew arrived or all would be ruined.

She found the spice seller, asked him for parsley, and handed over the coin he requested. It was likely far more than the spice was worth, but she didn't have the time – nor the inclination at the moment – to haggle with him.

Dried parsley in hand, she began to push back through the marketplace until she was near to rounding the corner.

She wondered where his parents had gone, for the house was not particularly large.

What was Matthew going to say when he saw her? Her heart started pounding as she wondered whether he would be surprised, excited, or disappointed. She was beginning to feel rather foolish about all she had planned. The thought that he might reject her was nearly too much for her to bear.

But she wouldn't focus on that. She would focus on—

"Hand over the reticule, and you will not be hurt."

Juliana stopped in her tracks, sharply inhaling.

Was this actually happening to her?

She surreptitiously reached her hand into the pocket at the front of her dress, slipping the knife into her hand before she slowly turned around, her eyes widening at the man in front of her. At his voice, she had envisioned someone who had clearly lived a life harder than one she could ever imagine. This man, however, appeared to be rather well put together. His dress wasn't so fine to be noble, but he had an air to him that told her this wasn't the first time he had stopped someone to take a few coins or jewels off them.

"I would be happy to give you the coins I can afford," she said calmly. "But I cannot give you all or else I might not be able to make my way home."

"A far cry from Mayfair, aren't you?"

Juliana tilted her head, eyeing him. He wore a black cloth with eye holes tied over his face so she couldn't properly see him, although she was having difficulty placing his accent. He didn't sound like any of the noblemen she knew, but nor did he seem to be a man without education. If she had to guess, he would be of similar class to Matthew, or to Dr. Lewis.

She hoped this didn't mean her half-brother had any involvement.

"Why would you believe I am from Mayfair?"

"The fancy dress, of course."

"Perhaps the same could be said for you."

The man scoffed before advancing to her menacingly. "Hand it over."

"Or what?"

"Or I will make things difficult for you," he said, brandishing a knife in his right hand.

Afterward, Juliana could only explain it as time having gone still. She saw him inch toward her even as she reviewed her options, trying to think through all that Matthew had taught her. Should she run? Should she fight? Should she use her weapon? First, she should be smart.

"Very well," she said calmly. "Take it."

It really was just a few coins, after all, and it was hardly worth potentially losing her life over. She held out the reticule with her left hand, and he reached out for it. Only, instead of taking the reticule, he snatched her wrist instead.

"What are you doing?" she asked, looking around wildly for help, only this corner was rather devoid of people. Of course.

He leaned in, his mouth widening into a sneer.

"I am taking the greatest prize of all," he said. "Do you think your brother will come for you again?"

Juliana was instantly awash with the ever-present fear that had been hanging just above her ever since the last time she had been abducted.

They had avoided anything like this ever happening to her again by having Matthew or one of his men shadow her every move. But Matthew wasn't here right now. It was just Juliana, against this man who threatened to take her back to the one place she had vowed to never be again – in captivity.

She had deliberately held the bag out in her left hand, and she flicked the knife up in her right hand, preparing to strike. She was already lashing out before he even saw it, and when she dug the weapon into his knife hand, his eyes widened in shock as he dropped the knife to the ground before them. A sickening dread dug into her stomach, but she didn't give herself time to realize exactly what she had done.

"What the—"

His surprise gave Juliana enough time to twist her hand in his grip, bringing her other arm down on top of his. Memories of her training with Matthew flashed through her mind, and she only hoped she could do enough to keep the man at bay.

He let out a yell, and before he could collect his wits and lash out for her again, Juliana did what Matthew had taught her – she ran.

She turned the corner and looked down the rows of doors in front of her. One of them was the Archibald residence, but which one? And if she went within, would she only be inviting trouble to their home? Just as she had decided that she must keep running past the door, a figure appeared at the other end of the street – one she would recognize anywhere.

"Matthew!" she yelled out in part-warning, part-relief, and she could tell when he saw her and the danger that threatened her, for his body crouched to ready for attack.

She instantly felt rather than saw the retreat of the man behind her, and she risked a glance over her shoulder to see him running the other way. She kept going, right into Matthew's arms, which she jumped into as soon as she was close. He wrapped them around her, holding her tight, and she could feel the beat of his heart as it thumped against her chest.

The warmth of his breath hit her ear, and she could tell how much the entire situation had affected him, even while she needed his comfort more than she ever had before. Juliana couldn't have said how long they stood there together, until he slowly eased away from her, setting her in front of him.

"What are you doing here? Why are you out in front of my parents' house alone?" he asked, his eyes still flitting back and forth from one side to the other as though he still wasn't prepared to give up on potential danger.

"I-I made something for you," she said, stepping back away from him, holding her hand out to him. "Come."

He nodded, his face inscrutable as he followed her through the front door of his parents' house. Neither Mrs. nor Mr. Archibald was anywhere to be seen, but Juliana's meal actually smelled half-decent.

"Sit," she said, pointing to the table, and he did as she said, although she could tell that his body wasn't entirely ready to relax.

She returned to the kitchen, found the spice that had mercifully survived her encounter, and added it to the soup. She looked at everything before her, and then began plating it for Matthew. If it hadn't been for the panicked beating of her heart, she thought she actually would have enjoyed herself and the ability to prepare food for the man she loved.

She walked from the kitchen holding their plates, placing one in front of him.

"What would you like to drink?"

He blinked at her, obviously still not understanding what was happening.

"Pardon me?"

"What would you like to drink?"

"Juliana, can we talk—"

"Please," she said desperately, "do not let him ruin this. We will talk later, I promise. But for now, what would you like to drink?"

"I'll get it," he said, and went to the sideboard to pour for himself, bringing them both back a glass of wine. He looked at the table in front of him.

"What is this?"

"You're the investigator," she couldn't help sniping at him. She was beginning to grow rather tired of being the one giving her all, while he continued to make what he considered his own damn sacrifice, but in reality was not her allowing to choose her own destiny. "Why do you not solve the case?"

"It looks like dinner."

"Yes. I made it for you," she said.

"Why?"

At that, Juliana had had enough. Between the events of tonight and his unwillingness to accept what she had done, she broke. She pushed away from the table before she had even finished sitting down, placing her fists upon it.

"Why? Because I wanted to show you that I am prepared to learn, to do this for you if it means a life together. That I love you and I don't care what that means. That I enjoy spending time with your family and would be happy to do so for the rest of our lives. But you, apparently, do not care. What else do I need to do to show you how I feel?"

"Juliana," he stood and rounded the table. "I know how you feel. I do."

"If you care so much about how I feel, then you will allow me to make my own decisions."

He reached out and placed his hands on her arms, his brow furrowed. "I appreciate this more than you know. Truly I do."

"Do not placate me."

"I am not."

"Do you believe it's any good? I made it all myself."

She lifted her chin in a challenge to him. He stared at her, meeting her gaze, though knew then he didn't have faith in her abilities.

He sat down as she knew he would, picking up his fork to stubbornly dig into his food. He stabbed his fork into the potatoes and brought it to his mouth. And she watched his eyes light up.

"This is good," he said, after he swallowed. She sat back, arms crossed over her chest.

"Surprised?"

"No."

"You are."

"Perhaps a bit."

She leaned in toward him. "I can do anything I put my mind to, Matthew. Never forget that."

His eyes were locked on her as he took a spoonful of the soup, then continued with the rest of his plate.

"I hope you do not miss the meat," she said as she tentatively tried a bite herself. "Your sisters said you were not eating it anymore."

"Maybe not."

"Why?"

He sighed. "Does it matter?"

"Yes."

"Because—because I read your pamphlet. And I listened at your meetings. And I discovered that there is much validity in your opinions."

"Did you, now?"

"Yes," he mumbled.

They ate the rest of the dinner in silence, although Juliana could see that his mind was working by the expressions that flitted across his face, knew that she had made a dent in his stubborn opinion on the matter of the two of them.

Finally, she brought out the dessert and he began to ask the questions he had been holding in.

"What could have happened to you tonight, alone out there?"

"I defended myself," she said. "And you know something? I needed to. I needed to know that I was strong enough to be able to stay safe without relying on you. Yes, it was your teaching that helped, but I fought that man off on my own."

"What if I hadn't come?"

"I would have found help. I would have kept running until I had found someone – anyone. If that wasn't an option, I would have fought him. I had my knife." She paused. "There is something you should know. That man was after me again for the same reason as before — for who I was. But I do not think it was the same man. I didn't recognize anything about him.

Matthew sighed as he ran his hands through his hair. "Well, one thing is for certain, then. It wasn't Lewis."

"No. Of that we can be certain."

"Good. Well, if that is all, I think it is time for me to go," she said, her heart breaking within her chest. She hated this polite, let's-be-friends attitude that Matthew seemed to have adopted. She would have all of him, or none of him at all. "I do nothing halfway, Matthew. You should know that. I'm leaving. Please clean the dishes so your mother doesn't have to."

She knew she should stay and help, but she supposed after all she had done and Matthew's apparent dismissal of it, the least he could do was wash the few remaining dishes. She was halfway out the door when she heard a shout from behind her. She turned to find Matthew hurrying toward her, and she wondered just what else he had to say.

"Juliana, stop," he called, and she couldn't help but do so. "Please."

She turned around, and a bit of hope sprang in her chest.

For if she wasn't mistaken, there was pleading in his eyes.

CHAPTER 27

Matthew's heart was thudding so hard he wondered if Juliana could hear it.

He was a man who planned. Who gathered all of the information available to him – and that he had to search for – before coming to a decision. But with Juliana, he continued to act on instinct, which more than unsettled him. It terrified him.

But he knew, without a doubt, what he had to do.

He reached out a hand, into which she slowly, tentatively, placed one of her own. He tugged on it, leading her deeper into the house, to the sitting room where he had grown up. He sank down to the couch, and she followed suit beside him.

He cleared his throat, intent on starting at the beginning to tell her of how he had gone to her house and found her missing, where her family had told him she was, her grandmother's warning, his own frenzied dash to his parents' house in complete shock, and then the furious mix of emotions that had coursed through him when he had turned the corner and saw her running toward him.

But he decided that wasn't the place to start – with Juliana there was only one place to do so.

"I love you," he said, putting great emphasis on each word, and yet still, they did not seem enough to truly describe the extent of what he felt for her. At the narrowing of her eyes, he knew she didn't believe him and he forged on, saying it louder, stronger. "I love you, with every part of me. I have never felt like this about a woman before, and I know I never will again. I just... I thought that my feelings weren't enough. I thought *I* wouldn't be enough for you, that this life would be one that you would grow to resent."

Her back straightened, her body stiffening, and he knew exactly what she was thinking.

He took both of her hands in his now as he sank to his knees in front of her, leaning his body forward as her eyes widened in surprise.

"But I realized something when we were apart, when I saw you running away from a man you defended yourself against, when you went to all this effort to make a meal for me in order to force me to see that there is no end to what you are capable of. I realized that it is not for me to make the decision for you. It is for you to understand what life would be like and then to determine for yourself if that is a life you would choose. I've been a stubborn fool, and while I cannot ask you to give up everything to be with me, I *will* tell you that I will no longer decide your future for you."

He finally looked up and met her eyes, squeezing her hands, trying to make her understand the truth to his words. Her eyes were glistening as she stared at him.

"Truly?"

He nodded. "Truly."

She sank down on to the floor next to him, wrapping her arms around his neck. "Then I choose you. Today, tomorrow, every day for the rest of our lives."

He reached out and captured her face between his hands.

"Will you marry me, then?"

"Of course I will," she said, her lips curling into a smile. "And I love you too."

He couldn't wait any longer then, as he dipped his head and took those smiling lips with his. The kiss started gentle, tender, loving, but before long she was grasping the lapels of his jacket, pulling herself up toward him as he delved into her mouth, tasting her, teasing her, and she returned it, giving as much as he did. He wasn't sure how it had happened, but soon she was straddling his lap, her legs wrapped around him as she brushed against him where he was straining toward her.

"Juliana," he murmured, breaking away. "Jules."

"Yes?"

"We have to stop."

"Why? We are getting married," she said, panting now as she pressed herself closer to him, bringing her lips to his again.

"Because we are in the middle of my parents' sitting room."

She froze before scrambling off his lap. "Right, right," she said, patting her hair back into some semblance of order. "That wouldn't be the best of impressions if they were to walk in, now would it?"

His laugh started as a low rumble before it spilled over, full of incredulity that it could be possible that this woman would become his wife.

"Let's clean up, shall we?" he said. "Then we will return home."

He didn't say which home, but then, he wasn't entirely sure himself.

"Where are my parents, anyway?"

It was at that moment that his mother appeared, and

Matthew didn't need to be an investigator to be suspicious of her timing.

"Matthew, how was your dinner?"

"It was wonderful, Mother."

"Thank you so much for allowing me to cook here, and, Mrs. Archibald, for all of your help," Juliana added, and Matthew could tell from his mother's fond gaze that Juliana had already won her over.

"It's getting late," his mother said. "Why don't you return Juliana home, Matthew, and I will clean up tonight?"

"Oh, no—" Juliana began, but his mother had held up her hand again.

"I insist," she said. "Go on, now. I am sure that Lady Juliana's family shall be waiting, and there might be a few things you need to discuss with her brother."

Of that, there was no doubt.

* * *

It was with a great amount of trepidation – and yet a great amount of joy – that Juliana and Matthew returned to Warwick House a short time later, after collecting Abigail on the way back.

Matthew was as stoic as ever, but Juliana could hardly contain the differing emotions within her.

"What do you think Giles will say?" she asked Matthew for what seemed to be the twentieth time since they had left his parents' house. The ever-loyal James had been waiting, and for the first time since Juliana had met him, Matthew sat in the carriage with her. She had tried her very best to tempt him on the way over, but he had resisted – barely – telling her that if they started anything he was not sure they would be able to stop.

THE SECRET OF THE DASHING DETECTIVE

She figured that was a good enough reason, and it was made much easier once Abigail joined them.

Jameson answered the door with raised eyebrows as he took in the two of them.

"Lady Juliana. You have returned. And with Mr. Archibald."

"Yes, Jameson," she said, unable to worry about the butler being cross with her, although his mood was usually a good indication of her mother's. "Where can we find Giles?"

"The family is partaking of their final dinner course," Jameson replied.

Juliana's heart sank. She should have realized the time. She would have much rather had this discussion with one family member at a time, although she supposed that perhaps having Emma and Prudence's support would not hurt. And, if what Matthew told her was any indication, it seemed that her grandmother was in their favor as well.

She looked down at her dress which, while fine by Holborn standards, would certainly not pass her mother's inspection for dinner. That was, of course, besides the fact that it was currently covered in a few splashes of food that had missed the apron while she was cooking. She lifted a hand to her hair, finding that as much of it had escaped its pins as was still hanging off her head.

But if her family was going to accept her marriage – and she certainly hoped they would – then they would have to accept her as she was.

She reached down and took Matthew's hand.

"We shall wait in the drawing room until they are finished."

Jameson lifted his eyebrows in a silent disapproval of her idea, but Juliana was not going to be discouraged. Did it truly matter if she was considered ruined now?

Matthew said nothing but gripped her hand tightly and followed her down. When they took a seat, she sighed and leaned into him, and he reached an arm around her shoulders and pulled her close.

"Do we have a plan?"

She closed her eyes and smiled at the fact that he was asking for her thoughts first.

"I suppose we shall explain all and then you will have to speak to Giles to ask for my hand."

"He might not give it."

"He might not," Juliana acquiesced. "But I am a grown woman, and I give it to you regardless."

She didn't like the idea of running away without approval any more than she knew Matthew did, but she refused to stay and marry the next man her mother chose for her just because that was expected.

Juliana was near to falling asleep from the excitement of the day when the door of the drawing room was nudged open and she jolted up in her seat.

"Juliana!"

It was Emma who entered first, thank goodness. She rushed in and leaned down to embrace Juliana. "We were worried about you when you didn't return before dinner."

"Juliana," Giles said from the doorway, where he stood with his arms folded over his chest. "I was about to send out a search party for you, to call on every armed man in London to find you, until our grandmother here gave me an inkling of where you were."

His eyes flicked over to Matthew. "Archibald."

"Your Grace," Matthew said, standing with a bow.

"It is true, then?" Juliana's mother said from where she stood just inside the entrance, hands clenched together in front of her bosom. "You were not with Lady Maria but rather... this man?"

"*This man*, Mother, has a name," Juliana said, setting her jaw, preparing for battle. "Matthew. And you best learn it well, for I intend to marry him."

Her mother gasped at that, turning to look to her own mother for assistance, but Lady Winchester only tapped her cane on the floor and smiled at Juliana. "Good for you, girl."

"Juliana, we must speak about this. There is so much more to consider than your simple infatuation. And you," she pointed at Matthew, "I told you to leave her be."

"I tried, Your Grace," Matthew said contritely. "Truly, I did."

"But wouldn't you know it, Matthew finally realized that I have my own mind," Juliana added.

"Giles, will you take care of this?" the dowager duchess said, turning to her son as her last resort, and Giles nodded, although his gaze was fixed on Matthew.

"Archibald, why do we not retreat to my study? It seems the two of us have a great deal to talk about."

Matthew leaned in and kissed Juliana's cheek, much to her surprise as well as everyone else's in the room, before he followed Giles out, leaving Juliana alone in the room with her sister gaping at her, her mother near to fainting, and both Emma and Lady Winchester wearing matching smiles of approval.

"I suppose you would all like to know what has happened?" she asked, and Emma nodded eagerly while the women finally found seats around the room.

She told them of how she had started developing feelings for Matthew, of how he had tried to resist her, of how their time together only brought them closer, until Matthew pushed her away for what he thought was forever.

Then she told them of the scheme she had concocted for the evening.

"And?" Prudence said, leaning forward, obviously captivated by her sister's story. "Did it work?"

"Yes," Juliana said with a smug smile. "It worked perfectly."

CHAPTER 28

Matthew was prepared to have a great deal of explaining ahead of him when he entered the duke's study. It had changed considerably since his first meeting here. Gone was the overbearing presence of the previous duke staring down at them from his portrait, the heavy navy curtains, the suffocating darkness of the room.

In its place was the brightness of what the duke's family was becoming.

Giles wearily took a seat behind his desk.

"If you were any other man or if Juliana was any other woman, I would instantly be suspicious of your motives. But my best guess is that you were the one who tried to resist this match and she would not allow it."

"That would be correct, Your Grace," Matthew said with a wry grin. "In case you are worried, however, I must tell you that I love her with all my heart. For that very reason I did try to break off any of the affection she had for me, but I did not see how strong her feelings were – that they were much more than affection but a returned love, in fact."

"Are you both aware of what she will be giving up by marrying you?"

"Yes, Your Grace," Matthew said. "In fact, that was one of the main reasons I tried to push her away. I wasn't sure that she was aware of what life awaited her if she were to marry me. But I was wrong. She knows her mind far better than I ever imagined. She was adamant that this is the life she chooses. She made quite a display of it, just in case I couldn't get it through my thick head."

He explained what Juliana had done that night, and Giles' eyebrows rose near to his hairline.

"I cannot say that I am pleased she lied to us all about her whereabouts, but... I am rather impressed."

Matthew nodded before continuing. "I would like to ask you for her hand. I know that I am far from what you would have expected or preferred for your sister, but I promise you that I will spend my life looking after her and providing her the best life I possibly can."

Giles eyed him for a moment before standing and rounding his desk, leaning back against it.

"I have a few questions."

"Of course."

"What if I do not provide you with her dowry?"

"I do not expect it, Your Grace. I am prepared to provide for Juliana without it."

"Are you able to?"

Matthew hid his ire. "Yes."

"Are you positive that you love her?"

Matthew paused for a moment — not because he needed to think about his answer, but because he needed to choose words that the duke would completely understand. In a low voice, he said, "With every piece of my heart and soul."

Giles nodded before returning to his seat.

"Good. I give you my blessing."

THE SECRET OF THE DASHING DETECTIVE

Matthew blinked, uncertain if he had actually just heard the duke correctly.

"Pardon me?"

"I said I give you my blessing. Are you what we expected for Juliana? No. Will my mother approve? No. But fortunately for you, I am not my father. I married for love myself, and while you may not be of noble birth, I know that you will make Juliana happy, which is more than I can say for most of the other potential matches my mother would have chosen for her. You not only have my blessing, but you have her dowry as well."

He turned around a sheet of paper and slid it across the desk to Matthew. Matthew read the number on it and was already shaking his head. The amount was more than he would make in five years, but he could not imagine accepting such a sum when he had done nothing to earn it.

"I cannot accept this, Your Grace."

"Of course you can," the duke said, eyeing him. "In fact, if you don't take it, I will remove my blessing."

"But... why?"

"Juliana's dowry is not for you. It is for her. While I have every bit of faith that you will provide for her, this will always be there for her if she needs it. You are not the type of man who will spend it all yourself, I know that. So use it to take care of her."

Matthew swallowed hard. It still stung to have to take the money, but he couldn't see any other way around it. He would just leave it to Juliana to do with as she pleased.

"Very well. Thank you, Your Grace."

"Now, we just have to determine the nuptials."

"Not to worry!"

The door flew open, and Juliana burst in. She rounded the desk and wrapped her arms around her brother's neck, obviously much to his surprise. "Thank you, Giles," she said.

"Thank you very much." She looked up and met Matthew's eyes. "And thank you, Matthew, for not fighting Giles on his wishes."

He nodded at her, knowing as he stared at for her that he would do anything she ever asked of him.

"This was to be a conversation between me and Mr. Archibald," Giles said dryly, to which his wife, standing near the door, snorted.

"You have been home long enough, Giles, to know that will never be the case."

He nodded before sighing.

"I suppose I do."

"As for the wedding," Juliana said, her eyes on Matthew, "I was thinking that perhaps we should get married at St. Andrew's."

"In Holborn?" Matthew asked with a raised eyebrow.

"Yes. It is where we shall live, is it not?"

They heard an exclamation from the hall that was clearly the dowager duchess, but Juliana didn't appear to have any time for that at the moment.

"As you wish," Matthew said, "but let us set the date for the near future, now, shall we?"

"Very well," Giles said.

"Before we continue, there is something else we must speak about," Matthew said, actually pleased they were all there so he wouldn't have to complete the story. "A man attempted to abduct Juliana tonight, and it was not Dr. Lewis who tried to do so."

"What?" Giles practically roared.

Matthew and Juliana explained the story as best and concisely as they could, but Giles was already pacing the floor.

"So we still have work to do," Matthew finished.

THE SECRET OF THE DASHING DETECTIVE

"Argh!" Giles said, kicking an umbrella stand in the corner that made all of the women jump.

"For what its worth, I will keep on it," Matthew said, "and not as a job. As a member of your family."

"Very good," Giles said grimly. "Thank you." He reached out his hand. "Brother."

* * *

THEY HAD AGREED to wait three weeks – the required three weeks for the banns to be read. Giles had offered to secure a special license for them to wed earlier and at Warwick House, but Juliana had insisted that she wanted to be married as they would be if her brother had not been a duke. It was the life she was going to be living soon, so she might as well start now, without any special privileges.

In those three weeks, Matthew had also given up his suite in the boarding house and found a small cottage in Holborn near to his parents' house – but not too near – and Juliana had spent a great deal of time along with Emma, Prudence, and Matthew's sisters in creating her own home. A home that was not extravagant by the standards she was used to, but was comfortable, and was hers – and Matthew's.

He walked her through the threshold now, a smile on his face that told her that he was up to something.

"Is this a good surprise or a bad surprise?" she asked with an eyebrow raised.

"What makes you think I have a surprise?"

"Perhaps you are not the only detective around here," she said with a smile.

He couldn't keep it within any longer, his mouth widening across his face as Juliana heard the scrambling of feet over the floor. She couldn't contain her glee as Lucy came running across the room and jumped into her waiting arms.

"Lucy!" she exclaimed before turning to Matthew in shock. "What is she doing here?"

"She's here to stay with us," Matthew said. "She's my wedding gift to you."

"This is—she is—you are—" Juliana was speechless. "This is incredible, Matthew. Thank you so much. I don't know what to say."

"You don't have to say anything," he said, reaching down and scooping Juliana up into his arms, dog and all. He walked her through the small house into their bedroom at the back, depositing her on the bed before gently taking Lucy from her arms and placing her onto the pallet on the floor he had made for her.

"Now come here, wife."

She squealed as he climbed overtop of her on the bed.

Juliana let her thighs fall open, welcoming him, and she smiled in appreciation for his exquisite form as he began to undress the top half of his body, until only a light smattering of hair covered his chest. She knew she was likely supposed to wait for him, but that wasn't in Juliana's nature. Instead, she lifted herself up from the bed and leaned in and kissed his collarbone on one side and then the other, feeling the fast beat of his pulse just below his skin.

"Jules," he groaned, her name a low rumble on his lips, and she liked it, this feeling of control over a man as strong as Matthew. She ran her hands over the muscles of his abdomen, kissing her way down his chest before leaning in, her nipples standing to attention when they brushed against his chest, even through the fabric covering them.

Matthew quickly made sure that was also out of the way as he pushed down her bodice and freed her breasts, before reaching behind her to try to untie the gown's elaborate fastenings.

He finally loosened the first one and then turned her over slightly to look at the rest and groaned aloud.

Juliana couldn't help but gasp when each clasp started to rip as he tore them all out.

"You will destroy the dress!" she exclaimed.

"I'll fix it," he muttered, before he pulled first the garment and then her chemise off her and leaned down, finally taking her lips. They had shared plenty of stolen kisses in the past few weeks, but this one was different. This was a thorough branding, a reminder of who she was now and who would be with her, every night, lying by her side.

He thrust his tongue into her mouth in a love play, and she moaned, especially when he began to squeeze her breasts with his large, rough palms.

"Thank goodness we were married today," he growled, "for I could not have spent another night without you in my bed."

He continued to ravage her mouth while his hands ran over her entire body, discovering new things that he seemed to like. She explored him in turn, until she reached the fall of his breeches and had to lean down and do her very best to unfasten them. She tried to ignore the fact that her fingers were shaking slightly, but he must have noticed for he eventually reached down to help her. When he was finally free, she found what she was looking for, closing her fingers around him, stroking him from root to tip. She had no idea if she was doing it right or not, but he threw back his head and began to groan so she figured something must feel good.

He didn't spend long simply enjoying, however, for before Juliana knew what was happening, his mouth was around one of her breasts, pulling, teasing, every piece of her body on edge, waiting. When he left one breast, he went to the next, using his fingers on the first so it didn't feel neglected.

She couldn't help but arch up into him, needing more, although this time she knew exactly what she wanted. His fingers slid from her breast, all the way down the front of her body, until they rested on the very place she yearned for him. Then Matthew parted her and began stroking in between her legs.

She continued to knead him in turn, satisfied to hear that his breath was coming as fast and as hard as her own.

A throbbing began between her legs, which he answered by brushing over the small spot that seemed to make her feel absolutely everything. He slipped a finger into her and she moaned, which seemed to be enough for him. She lifted her hips up to him, ready for him to give her something besides his fingers, but instead he rocked them into her a few more times until she went over the edge, her entire world exploding and then coming back together again.

He began to whisper in her ear, words that she knew no lady should hear, but then, she was not just any lady, now was she? She had proven that today.

"You are perfection," he said, as he seemed fascinated by her breasts in front of him, and she strained up toward him, letting him take his fill. He shifted so that he was right between her legs, his cock probing against her.

"Are you ready?"

"Absolutely," she said enthusiastically, and then he began to slide into her with a long groan. Juliana pulled her knees up to allow him easier access.

"You are so tight," he said with a groan.

"I'm sorry."

"No!" he practically shouted. "It's a good thing. Am I hurting you?"

Juliana shook her head rapidly. If she thought he had been

panting before, now he could barely catch his breath. He began to pull out and then push in, slowly at first, until Juliana responded with a grin and told him now amazing it was. Now that she had relaxed around him, it began to feel better and better, until tears were leaking out of her eyes at the exquisiteness. She let her nails press into the tops of his shoulders as he began to move faster and faster still until the sensation inside of her was building again. He must have sensed it, for he leaned down into her as his hard chest rubbed against her breasts.

"I love you," he groaned, and then with one final plunge, he shouted her name and she lost control again as she allowed the indescribable sensations to take over. He rocked in and out a few more times until he stilled, not moving within her at all as they revelled in what they had just experienced.

They held each other as they came down from their high, until they were left lying together, sated, with their torn wedding clothes scattered around them.

"There is one thing I can tell you with all certainty," Juliana said, turning her head to look at him with a smile.

"What's that?" he asked, rolling onto his side and wrapping an arm around her.

"There is nothing that can be better than that. Not even lily-scented hot baths or jewel-encrusted gowns, or meals created by a French chef. Thank you."

"Why you are very welcome," he said with a grin as he winked at her. "Now, if you liked it so much, why don't we do it again?"

And they did.

EPILOGUE

TWO WEEKS LATER

There had been a few instances when Matthew had been nervous walking into Warwick House. Namely, when he came to see Juliana knowing he loved her but didn't think he could have her, and when he and Juliana had come to declare their love to her family.

But tonight, he was nervous for an altogether different reason.

He looked over at the woman on his arm. His wife.

"What do you think?" he asked, his heart in his throat. "Do you miss this?"

She turned from him to look up at Warwick House, the smile remaining on her face one of happiness and joy, with no note in her expression of any regret or longing.

"The only thing I miss is seeing Emma and Prudence every day," she said. "But the fact that I am able to spend much of my days – and *all* of my nights – with you makes up

THE SECRET OF THE DASHING DETECTIVE

for it. Besides, I visit them nearly as often as Emma used to visit me before we lived together."

Matthew squeezed her arm into his side. "I am glad to hear it."

"And also, our house is so full that I hardly have time to think about how things have changed."

Matthew chuckled at that. He had known that Lucy would come with Juliana. What he hadn't known was that Lucy was only the beginning. In only two weeks their family had already grown to add the big shaggy dog who Juliana called Max, two cats, one missing an ear and the other a leg, and a magpie who apparently couldn't fend for itself in the wild. It often flew away and Matthew kept hoping it would find a home elsewhere.

But it continued to come back, often delighting Juliana with pretty stones and trinkets.

"Does your mother know we are attending tonight?" Matthew asked as he knocked and waited for Jameson to allow them entrance.

"She does," Juliana said with a nod. "And she has promised to be on her best behaviour."

The dowager duchess had not yet quite come around to accepting their marriage. She had no choice but to accept it when Giles had, but she had sat in the front row of their nuptials with her arms crossed over her chest and a glower on her face to make it clear she was not in favor of the match.

Juliana didn't seem to care, so Matthew tried not to let it bother him either.

"It's Prudence's birthday, so she chose the guest list," Juliana said as the door swung open. "We must all agree to it."

Jameson's nod tonight was one of respect, and he took their cloaks before leading them through and into the drawing room.

"Jules!" Emma and Prudence were the first to greet them, immediately taking Juliana off with them, leaving Matthew to greet the duke and the other guest who was with him.

"Dr. Lewis," Matthew said, pleasantly shocked. "It's good to see you."

Lewis took his hand. "And you, Archibald. I have much to thank you for."

"In the end, I didn't have to do much to clear your name," Matthew said. "It resolved on its own, although not without putting Juliana in some peril."

"Which I was sorry to hear about," Lewis said, his words honest. "But I do wish you my very best on your marriage. A marriage in truth this time."

He and Matthew were able to laugh about that now, with the duke seeming somewhat chagrined.

"I have begun to make my apologies to Dr. Lewis," the duke said, although when Matthew looked over at Lewis, he didn't seem entirely convinced. "Now we have to determine where the true threat lies."

The door opened behind Matthew's shoulder, and the duke looked over with a smile of welcome. Matthew's eyes shifted to Lewis then, and that was when he was truly surprised. For Lewis seemed... enraptured. Matthew turned to see just what – or who – had captured his attention.

"Lady Maria, how good to see you!" Matthew was distracted by Juliana, who drifted by him to greet her new friend. She led her into the room, her mother following behind with a curious expression on her face.

"I wasn't sure if we should have come, with all that has occurred in your family as of late," Lady Bennington was saying to the dowager duchess. "But you are such good friends of the family and all."

The dowager duchess and Lady Hemingway, who had also

been invited this evening, Matthew noted, exchanged a knowing glance. Matthew looked around for Lord Hemingway, grateful when he didn't see him. It was not that he had anything against the man. It was just that it was rather awkward to see him after all that had happened. The fact he had been in attendance at their wedding hadn't helped matters.

"As it happens, Lady Bennington, all is well in hand," the duke said smoothly, even though his words were far from the truth. "Our family is safe, our house is one of the best protected in London, and we are closer to one another than we have ever been. We are pleased to welcome you and Lady Maria into our home."

She nodded, although her eyes wandered to first Matthew and then to Lewis – making it more than obvious that she didn't appreciate Matthew's presence, but then she tilted her head in curiosity.

"I believe I have only seen this gentleman in passing – a few weeks ago, in this very house," she said, with a smile for him.

"This is Dr. Lewis," the duke said, and opened his mouth to continue, but Lewis cut in before he could.

"I am a friend of the family," he said smoothly, which was likely the smartest decision. It would be in no one's best interests to make known the true nature of his origin.

She paused for a moment before a polite smile crossed her face, as she likely wondered what a physician was doing here but knew she could not so question a duke.

"Pleased to meet you," she said. "May I introduce my daughter, Lady Maria?"

Lady Maria turned at her name, and Matthew noted the way her eyes fixated on Lewis.

"We have met in passing," she finally said. "It is wonderful to see you again, Dr. Lewis."

"The same to you, my lady," he said, dipping into a bow before the duke finally broke the tension.

"A drink, Lewis?"

"A drink," he confirmed, and Matthew turned to join them, but found Juliana at his side.

"That was interesting," she murmured as he led her to the side of the room.

"So it was," he said with a nod.

"Lady Maria is so beautiful that it would be hard *not* to notice her," Juliana said.

Matthew tucked his hand around her waist.

"There is only one woman in this room whose beauty enraptures me so."

"Oh?" she said coyly. "And who would that be?"

"A certain Mrs. Archibald."

"She's a lucky woman," Juliana said as he led her into the shadows and she wrapped her arms around his neck, leaning in close. "A lucky woman indeed."

THE END

* * *

Dear reader,

I hope you enjoyed reading Juliana and Matthew's across-class, bodyguard romance! There is still much left to uncover in the Warwick family mystery, but we will leave that to our next two books in the series to solve. Wondering about the undeniable connection between Lady Maria and Dr. Lewis – and whether the "diamond" of the *ton* could ever be with a bastard? You can find out in the next book, *The Clue of the Brilliant Bastard*, which is available on Amazon.

A quick word on some of the history that inspired this story. Juliana's vegetarian society may seem slightly ahead of its time – which is both true and false. While a formal Vegetarian Society would not emerge until 1847, vegetarians and animal rights activities have been noted since the early 1800s. John Newton published *Return to Nature: Or a Defence of the Vegetable Regimen* in 1811, who included the research of William Lambe. He influenced Percy Shelley to become a vegetarian. Shelley published *A Vindication of Natural Diet* in 1813.

There is much more fascinating reading available.

If you haven't yet signed up for my newsletter, I would love to have you join us! You will receive Unmasking a Duke for free, as well as links to giveaways, sales, new releases, and stories about my coffee addiction, my struggle to keep my plants alive, and how much trouble one loveable wolf-lookalike dog can get into.

www.elliestclair.com/ellies-newsletter

Or you can join my Facebook group, Ellie St. Clair's Ever Afters, and stay in touch daily.

Until next time, happy reading!

With love,
Ellie

* * *

The Clue of the Brilliant Bastard
Remingtons of the Regency Book 3

SHE WAKES **up in the arms of the very man she can never have. Will their forbidden love ever survive all that threatens them?**

Lady Maria has always done as she is told – until the former Diamond of the First Water faces a husband of unspeakable cruelty and escapes out a window and into the night, waking in the arms of the physician who affects her as no other man has.

When Lady Maria shows up on his doorstep, injured, frightened, and alone, Dr. Hudson Lewis cannot help but look after her – even if it means sacrificing his heart to resist temptation. For he, a duke's bastard, will never be good enough for a woman like Lady Maria – especially after he has been accused of murdering his father.

To protect Maria, Hudson must set aside his pride and turn to his half-siblings, the Remingtons, for help. When danger threatens, they are all at risk, and must work together to stay safe and determine who is pursuing them. Will Hudson and Maria's hearts be able to withstand all that is against them?

The Clue of the Brilliant Bastard is the heart-pounding steamy third book in the Remingtons of the Regency series. If you enjoy forbidden love, across class romance, gentlemen heroes, and women standing up for themselves, then you'll love Ellie St. Clair's intriguing romance. While the romance is a standalone, this series is best read in order.

THE CLUE OF THE BRILLIANT
BASTARD - CHAPTER ONE

*M*aria could not stop her shaking.

She fisted her hands together, wrapping her fingers tightly around one another, feeling the hateful ring biting into her skin. She longed to rip it off, to throw it across the church along with the vows that had just been uttered from her very own lips.

But it was too late. It was done.

She was married.

She couldn't look up at the man next to her. She hardly knew him, and wondered if she should have attempted to become better acquainted with him before they had actually wed – although it was a little late for that now. He had courted her as was expected, yes, but it had been nothing more than a dance when they attended the same event, tea with her mother present, and a ride through Hyde Park. It was all a farce, if anyone were to ask Maria.

But, of course, no one did.

She smiled woodenly at all of the people who had gathered in St. George's to witness the carefully contrived match.

One that her parents were ever so pleased with, especially when they had despaired of their daughter ever finding a respectable husband after been turned aside by a duke for a woman most considered quite odd and not at all marriageable.

Maria actually quite liked Lady Emma – now the Duchess of Warwick – but of course, that was of no consequence to anyone either.

So she did what she always did. She smiled and nodded.

All in attendance seemed quite approving of the match. All but her friend, Juliana, who stared at her now with the same concern she had expressed before the wedding, concern that Maria had tried to brush away.

She couldn't have said how she walked down the aisle, out of the church, and climbed into the carriage, but suddenly she realized she was sitting within it on the squabs, alone with her husband. A stranger.

He leaned toward her, coming perilously close to her face. She tried not visibly bristle at the warmth of his breath on her cheek, nor the odour that accompanied it, which she felt was akin to cheap ale mixed with salmon that had gone putrid and sat in the icebox for far too long.

"Alone at last."

Maria swallowed hard, keeping her gaze on the top of the squab across from her, wishing she was sitting upon it and not beside the man who was now her husband.

Her husband. How was it that despite the fact this had been expected of her for her entire life, it still seemed such a foreign concept?

Before she knew what was happening, his large hand was on her thigh, squeezing, rising along her leg, and Maria held her breath as she willed him away – but of course, that did nothing to stop him, as his hand ran higher until—

"Stop!" she yelped, jumping away across the seat.

She slapped a hand over her mouth when she caught her husband's glare. His eyes were harsh, his lips curled into a snarl, and the face that most in society considered handsome became twisted into a villainous expression that made her curl into the corner as though she could hide from him.

"I-I'm sorry," she stammered before he could say anything. "I was startled, and th-this is all quite sudden, and I—"

She didn't know what else to say. For she knew what she was supposed to do. Her mother had been very clear about what the expectations of her husband would be. Maria's stomach had churned at the thought of having to give control of her body to a man she didn't even know, but her mother had been very clear that she had no other choice.

But now that it was about to become reality, her acceptance of the fact no longer seemed as rational as it had been while sitting in her own bedroom and contemplating what was to come.

"You are my wife," her husband bit out, advancing on her once more. "I can do as I please, and there is nothing that you have to say about it. Do you understand me?"

Maria, always one to quickly agree to what was spoken to her, found that for once, she didn't have it within herself to accept what he said.

"I-I understand, however, perhaps, I could have some time."

"Time for what?"

"To become accustomed to being married. To come to know you better. To—"

To her surprise, he let out a laugh. Only it wasn't a laugh of mirth. It was a long, cruel laugh, one that told her he would have no mercy on her, would not accept anything she had to say.

He leaned in close to her once more. "I'm not sure what

you think this is all about," he said, "but I will have what I want, when I want it. Now, since you have not allowed me a taste, I shall have much more pent-up... desire tonight. You can have your *time*. But it runs out when the sun goes down."

Then he grinned, a slow, evil spreading of his lips that sent shivers all the way down Maria's spine.

Perhaps she was imagining things. Her husband was a man of rank, one who society accepted and seemed to admire. He certainly looked the part of the English gentleman with his light curled hair, perfectly coiffed, the sideburns sculpted to an exacting length, the crisp, expensive clothing.

Perhaps this was how every bride felt in anticipation of what was to come on her wedding night. But then she remembered asking her friend, Juliana, about what she should expect. Juliana's smile had been nothing short of smug and saucy, as she told Maria that coming together with a man one loved was more than she could ever have dreamed.

But Juliana had chosen her husband. She had risked everything for him, as he was nothing more than a detective and she the sister of a duke. Maria knew she could never be strong enough to do the same.

A niggling thought tugged at her – one of a certain physician, the son of a duke, yes, but a bastard son. One who she had only met a couple of times, but who had made her heart beat faster than it ever had before.

But he was not for her. No, her father had promised her to Lord Bradley Dennison, and whatever she desired, whatever Maria had thought she had wanted, was no longer an option.

For she was now Lady Dennison, and it was too late for her.

All she could do now was obey.

~~~~~

"Hudson?"

Hudson Lewis had just finished tidying his tools following the visit with his previous patient. As a physician, he was expected to simply diagnose, but he preferred to take more of a hands-on approach than most of his peers. For major operations, he referred his patients to a surgeon, one he trusted, but if it was a small ailment he could treat himself, he would do so.

"Yes?" he responded to his mother, who often accompanied him on his visits, assisting him as necessary. She had followed him home, as she often remained until he was most likely to be finished for the day.

She opened the door of the small study he used as his office, her greying head poking through.

"Do you have a moment?"

"Of course."

She slipped through the door as though she was attempting to surreptitiously hide from someone, closing it quickly behind her before leaning back against it.

"You have a visitor," she said, her voice so low that it was near to a whisper.

"That is the nature of my business," he couldn't help but say wryly, and she shot him a glare. "And for your role here – to assess who has come to fetch me. Is the case urgent?"

"Not a patient. A *visitor*."

Hudson eyed her with some annoyance. "Would you care to tell me who it is?"

"It's one of *them*."

"I am assuming from the vehemence in your voice that it is a member of the duke's family."

"Somewhat."

He sighed, about to tell his mother to either come out and tell him what she wished to say or to leave and send in his next patient.

"It's Matthew Archibald."

The voice, however, was not his mother's. It came from the other side of the door, and sounded a great deal like Archibald himself.

"Mother, the walls of this house are thin," he said, crossing his arms over his chest. Nor were the doors particularly thick.

His mother was correct, in a way, however. Matthew Archibald may not have been a member of the duke's family, but he was married to one – the duke's sister.

His own half-sister.

Hudson still had a difficult time believing that he was related to a duke and his family, that he was the son of a man who had been one of the most powerful in the country.

He had always known he was a bastard, however. That certainly hadn't changed.

"Come in, Archibald," he called out. The detective wasn't a bad sort, and despite his role in the investigation into the previous duke's death, he had risked everything to clear Hudson's name when he had been suspected of his murder.

"Lewis," Archibald said, reaching out to shake his hand, which Hudson took while his mother looked on with disapproval in her eyes. He understood her hesitancy in trusting anyone related to the Remington family – she had been turned out years ago when she, a maid, had became pregnant with the duke's bastard – but she must understand that Archibald had none of the sins of the duke on his hands.

He had simply been hired to look into his death, and in the process, had fallen in love with the man's daughter.

"Is this a social call?" Lewis asked, raising an eyebrow. As much as he enjoyed Archibald's company, he did have patients to see.

"You could say that," Archibald said, casting a glance over at Hudson's mother, but she appeared rooted to the spot, apparently not leaving until she knew what Archibald was here to say. "I come with an invitation as well as a message."

He held a note out to Hudson, who took it from his hand. He scanned the message before looking up at Hudson with raised eyebrows.

"The Duchess of Warwick invites me to a ball?"

"She does," Archibald said, ignoring Hudson's mother, who let out a snort that was not only undisguised but clearly on purpose for him to hear.

"No thank you," Hudson said, handing the invitation back, but Archibald raised his hands in the air.

"That is why I'm here. With the message. Emma understands why you might not want to come, but the entire family wanted you to know that they would very much appreciate your presence at the event. I know there was an unfortunate circumstance—"

"They accused my son of murder!" Hudson's mother burst in, and Hudson closed his eyes for a moment and pinched the bridge of his nose.

"Mother," he said as gently as he could, "perhaps Mr. Archibald and I might have a moment alone to discuss this."

"But—"

"I promise you I am perfectly capable of speaking for myself."

She let out a "humph," but finally left the room, which allowed Hudson a sigh of relief.

"She does not have the best delivery," Hudson said to Archibald, "but she is right. The family – the duke in particular – did accuse me of murder. Despite evidence that spoke otherwise."

"I know," Archibald said, "but it was primarily the duke's accusations."

"And his mother's."

"That is true. But Juliana, Emma, and Prudence – as well as their grandmother, Lady Winchester – were all very much in support of you."

"Which I am grateful for. But I hardly think society will willingly accept my presence."

"That, I understand," Archibald said, lifting his hat and raking a hand through his straight, light brown hair. "As it happens, there is an event ongoing today that I am not invited to myself, being a detective and all and not appropriate for such company."

"Oh?" Hudson said, though not at all interested. "Did Juliana attend without you?"

"She did," Archibald said with a nod, no emotion on his face. "She didn't want to, in protest for my omittance from the guest list, but we both knew how much her presence meant to Maria and—"

"Maria?"

Hudson couldn't stop his reaction as his head snapped up and mention of her name.

Archibald's eyebrows rose and Hudson cleared his throat as he turned his back and made a farce of tending to his instruments once more.

"I made Lady Maria's acquaintance some time ago," Hudson said, "and have not seen her in a few months. She was very... polite. I wondered how she was getting on."

He was well aware that it was far too much of an explanation, but once he had started his ramble, he wasn't sure where to stop.

"Yes," Archibald said, as Hudson turned his head over his shoulder to look at him. "It was her... event after all."

"Her event?" Hudson said, feigning nonchalance.

"You could call it that," Archibald said, pausing for a moment before telling him the truth of it all. "Lady Maria is getting married today."

Find The Clue of the Brilliant Bastard on Amazon and in Kindle Unlimited.

ALSO BY ELLIE ST. CLAIR

The Remingtons
The Mystery of the Debonair Duke
The Secret of the Dashing Detective
The Clue of the Brilliant Bastard
The Quest of the Reclusive Rogue

To the Time of the Highlanders
A Time to Wed
A Time to Love
A Time to Dream

Thieves of Desire
The Art of Stealing a Duke's Heart
A Jewel for the Taking
A Prize Worth Fighting For
Gambling for the Lost Lord's Love
Romance of a Robbery

The Bluestocking Scandals
Designs on a Duke
Inventing the Viscount
Discovering the Baron
The Valet Experiment
Writing the Rake
Risking the Detective
A Noble Excavation

<u>A Gentleman of Mystery</u>

The Bluestocking Scandals Box Set: Books 1-4
The Bluestocking Scandals Box Set: Books 5-8

Blooming Brides
A Duke for Daisy
A Marquess for Marigold
An Earl for Iris
A Viscount for Violet

The Blooming Brides Box Set: Books 1-4

Happily Ever After
The Duke She Wished For
Someday Her Duke Will Come
Once Upon a Duke's Dream
He's a Duke, But I Love Him
Loved by the Viscount
Because the Earl Loved Me

Happily Ever After Box Set Books 1-3
Happily Ever After Box Set Books 4-6

The Victorian Highlanders
Duncan's Christmas - (prequel)
<u>Callum's Vow</u>
<u>Finlay's Duty</u>
<u>Adam's Call</u>
<u>Roderick's Purpose</u>
<u>Peggy's Love</u>

The Victorian Highlanders Box Set Books 1-5

Searching Hearts

Duke of Christmas (prequel)

Quest of Honor

Clue of Affection

Hearts of Trust

Hope of Romance

Promise of Redemption

Searching Hearts Box Set (Books 1-5)

Standalones

Always Your Love

The Stormswept Stowaway

A Touch of Temptation

Christmastide with His Countess

Her Christmas Wish

Merry Misrule

A Match Made at Christmas

For a full list of all of Ellie's books, please see www.elliestclair.com/books.

ABOUT THE AUTHOR

Ellie has always loved reading, writing, and history. For many years she has written short stories, non-fiction, and has worked on her true love and passion -- romance novels.

In every era there is the chance for romance, and Ellie enjoys exploring many different time periods, cultures, and geographic locations. No matter when or where, love can always prevail. She has a particular soft spot for the bad boys of history, and loves a strong heroine in her stories.

Ellie and her husband love nothing more than spending time at home with their children and Husky cross. Ellie can typically be found at the lake in the summer, pushing the stroller all year round, and, of course, with her computer in her lap or a book in hand.

She also loves corresponding with readers, so be sure to contact her!

www.elliestclair.com
ellie@elliestclair.com

Ellie St. Clair's Ever Afters Facebook Group

TRACY

Printed in Great Britain
by Amazon